TWO FOR JOY

A Magpie Romantic Suspense Mystery

Marlow Kelly

Viceroy Press

ISBN: 978-1-9991430-7-7

Edited by Corinne Demaagd
From CMD Writing and Editing
https://cmdediting.com

Proofreading by
Gemma Brocato
https://www.gemmabrocato.com

For news of Marlow's next release sign up for Marlow's Newsletter at:
www.marlowkelly.com

CHAPTER ONE

The cat burglar scrambled up the rain-soaked drainpipe and then reached for the open window on the second floor. It was nine at night, half an hour before dusk, which meant he was more exposed than usual. But he'd agreed to follow his contact's instructions to the letter. Luckily, the rear of the house on Sycamore Street faced the Bow River and was hidden by trees, which meant he couldn't be seen by passersby. He'd caught a break with the weather, too. The low-hanging clouds and light drizzle also helped obscure him.

He paused with one hand on the windowsill when the guests attending the dinner party downstairs fell silent. When they burst into laughter, he smiled. Everything was going according to plan.

He eased himself into a sitting position on the ledge and then pulled his legs up to his chest. He spun so he faced the interior of a large bedroom. It contained a king-sized bed, two nightstands, and a dresser. Unfortunately, the walls were white, and the floors were a light-colored hardwood. He was dressed in black from head to toe, even down to his latex gloves. This normally allowed him to blend into the dusky shadows. Not this time.

The mansion was situated in the heart of Banff, a tourist town in the Canadian Rockies. The multimillion-dollar residence was rare in this town since the expansion of the town limits was strictly prohibited due to the fact that it was smack dab in the middle of Banff National Park, a UNESCO World Heritage Site.

He crept across the floor, ignoring the diamond ring that sat on the nightstand beside the bed. He didn't want to be obvious. There was a good chance the owner would notice immediately if the piece was missing. It was better if they didn't realize they'd been robbed until tomorrow.

He opened the door to the linen cupboard, cringing when the hinges creaked, and then rummaged through the folded satin sheets. Finally, at the bottom of the pile, he touched something hard. He carefully untangled a small plain wooden box. Hidden inside was an emerald and diamond necklace with matching earrings. He stuffed the jewels into his backpack and returned the box and the sheet to their hiding place.

He glanced down the hallway to the left. The door to the master bedroom was shut. That room held a safe behind a Monet reproduction, but that could wait until later. First, he had to keep his appointment. Justin Cross had contacted him using one of his message boards, and had provided him with a layout of the house along with important details that were necessary for his work.

He edged along the darkened hallway, moving silently until he reached the third door on the right. Holding his breath, he listened as the people downstairs continued their conversation. Once he was convinced they were occupied, he turned the handle and stepped inside, inching the door closed behind him. An earthy, fetid stench stung his nostrils. He covered his nose and breathed through his mouth in an attempt to block out the foul odor. He dismissed the smell, concentrating on the job instead. Even mansions must have plumbing problems.

Despite the opulence of the house, the office was small. An oversize wooden desk with a matching chair was positioned at the far end in front of a tiny high-set window. Two weird pink armchairs sat in front of the desk, and a long side table was against the wall on his left. A small lamp illuminated the desk, casting long shadows on the pale walls. He'd expected his contact, Justin Cross, assistant to the CFO of Starling Stores, to be here. Perhaps he'd been delayed.

He took another step forward, then stopped cold and listened. He heard a low wheezing above the electrical buzz of the lamp. Huge splashes of blood stained the large rug that covered the floor. His stomach heaved at the sight. Every fiber in his body told him to run, but his macabre curiosity made him stay. He followed the grizzly trail that led behind the desk.

Justin lay in a heap on the floor. A wet, gooey mass dribbled down his neck from a gash to the back of his head.

"No." The sound had been a reflex. He clamped a hand over his mouth to stop making more noise as his mind scrambled to cope with what he was seeing.

He kneeled at Justin's side and felt his neck for a pulse. There was a faint rhythm.

Justin's eyes fluttered as he groaned.

"What happened?" He heard the tremble in his own voice.

"Take it," Justin rasped.

"Take what?" He looked into Justin's gaze but wished he hadn't. The dying man's dark eyes conveyed fear, desperation, and sadness.

Justin took two more labored breaths and whispered, "Hand."

"Never mind that. We need to get you help."

"Hand." Justin wheezed again and then fell silent. His eyes went blank, and every bone, every muscle in his body, seemed to slump.

He checked Justin's neck, feeling for a pulse again, but there was nothing. If only he'd arrived a few minutes earlier, he might have been able to save him.

He wasn't a religious man, but he said a small prayer, hoping that if heaven existed, Justin would end up there. Then he pried Justin's fingers open and retrieved a red and gold memory stick from the dead man's hand.

He stood and rubbed his beard as he glanced around the room.

The desktop was empty. There were no papers, nothing. He shone his flashlight over the edge of the desk. It was clear. Then he examined the small side table. Bingo. Somehow Justin's head had hit the corner, which now shone red with blood. Once hurt, instead of calling for help, he had crawled behind the desk, probably to retrieve the USB drive.

The people downstairs laughed again. The sound forced him to think about the reality of the situation. No one would believe he hadn't killed Justin. He needed to leave.

He checked the room, making sure he hadn't left any evidence behind. Then he opened the door with the same care he'd used when he entered and backtracked through the house.

As he reached for the ledge in the spare room, he noticed his hands were shaking. *Hold it together.*

He shimmied down the drainpipe and disappeared into the trees.

CHAPTER TWO

Georgina woke to the salt-laden, meaty smell of bacon cooking. She sat up in bed and stretched her arms over her head as she gave a jaw-popping yawn. Then she collapsed back onto her pillow. She wasn't ready to face the day, or maybe she didn't want to deal with Liam. She tugged the quilt over her head and was instantly enveloped with his scent. *Big mistake.*

He'd returned last night after a two-month absence. She was ecstatic he was back, but she wasn't sure where she stood with him. Their relationship before he left, if you could call it that, had been a whirlwind, spur-of-the-moment thing. They had met when he was working undercover as a police officer with the Magpie Police Service. He had been sent to the small town of Magpie, Alberta, to discover who was stealing drugs from the evidence locker and passing them to George's father, the local drug dealer. The culprit turned out to be a civilian employee, Lillian Field. Liam, who was actually a corporal with the Royal Canadian Mounted Police, had cleared George's name and arrested her criminal father.

They hadn't discussed their future or their plans before he'd left to work another undercover assignment. Now that he was back, everything felt real. What they'd shared in June hadn't been a fling for her, but it all had happened so fast. She'd fallen for him hard, and then he'd been whisked away onto his next job.

She couldn't be certain he'd returned because he wanted to be in a relationship with her. Maybe he'd just come back for sex and planned to take off again, or maybe not. They hadn't made love last night. He hadn't initiated it, and neither had she.

The problem was she had no idea what either of them wanted. She could ask, but her own feelings were a mystery, so it wouldn't do any good.

Her stomach knotted. Suddenly, the bacon wasn't so enticing. She was overthinking things. She should relax and take it minute by minute, day by day. If they couldn't get along in the present, then they had no future together. It was as simple as that.

Okay, problem solved. She would live in the moment. She was relieved they hadn't been intimate last night. It was too soon for her. She needed to get used to him again. Plus, he'd seemed totally exhausted when he'd knocked on her door. As if every ounce of energy had been wrung out of him.

She climbed out of bed and padded to the kitchen, still wearing her oversize white T-shirt that came to her upper thighs. Her house was small with just a bedroom, bathroom, living room, and kitchen. Most of her furniture was second-hand. She'd refinished the coffee table, chest, and hutch herself, a hobby that she'd abandoned after the death of her friend Smokey.

Liam patted the bacon with a paper towel and then smiled at her. His dark eyes shone as they roamed her figure. "Hi."

He wore a pair of khaki cargo shorts and a faded black T-shirt with a heavy metal logo on the front. The fabric stretched across his muscled shoulders. An ugly black and purple bruise on his left bicep poked out beneath the short sleeve.

Heat flooded her body at his naked interest. Perhaps it wasn't too soon for her to be intimate with him. It took all her energy to suppress the overwhelming urge to touch him and feel his warm, toned flesh under her fingertips. She refused to play mind games and pretend she didn't want him because she did, and when he was ready, she'd be there.

"Hi yourself. How are you feeling this morning? I thought you'd sleep in." She pressed her lips together to stifle the impulse to pepper him with questions about how he'd been hurt.

"Me, too." He set the plate in the middle of the table. There was another welt on his forearm. "My mind started going, and I couldn't get back to sleep. I figured I'd take a nap this afternoon." Dark circles shadowed his eyes, and the lines around his mouth seemed deeper than they had been in June. His dull gaze revealed his fatigue.

She gave him a bright smile, hoping to lighten his mood. "Sounds like a plan. Is that coffee I smell?"

"Of course." He grinned, but it didn't reach his eyes. "You have an awful lot of coffee-making equipment, but no toaster. I had to use your broiler."

Whatever had happened to him in the last two months had cost him. "A girl has to have her priorities." She filled a mug and placed it on her small kitchen table.

"I guess toast isn't a priority." He added a plate of eggs to the bacon and toast that was already there.

She laid a place for each of them. "Toast is just warm bread, so I've never bothered."

He laughed as he took a seat. She joined him and was about to tuck in when he covered her hand with his. "I never asked, how did your tests go?"

He was talking about the EEG, CT scan, and MRI, which had been ordered after she'd had a seizure triggered by a concussion. She'd been injured on the job while Liam had been posing as her partner.

With her free hand, she squeezed her thumb and index finger together. "I have a teeny weenie scar on my brain. That's what caused the seizure."

He released her hand and scooped some eggs onto his plate, along with a generous amount of bacon. "Are you on medication?" He obviously knew that for most epilepsy sufferers', seizures were controlled with treatment.

"No, I'm in a wait-and-see mode. The scar might disappear. Only twenty-five percent of people who have an early post-traumatic seizure will have another one." That fact had become her mantra. A small kernel of hope she clung to, praying the episode had been a one-off event, and after six months without an attack, she could get her driver's license back, maybe even her job as a cop. Her appetite had disappeared but she added a spoonful of eggs and half a slice of toast to her plate.

"You're saying it might all go away." His lips turned up at the corners in a fake smile.

"I'm hoping." She moved the eggs around with her fork.

"Are you back at work?" He bit down on a strip of bacon.

"No. I doubt they'd give me my old job back. I just don't see how they could take the risk that I wouldn't have a fit."

He finished chewing and said, "A desk it is then."

She piled a small amount of egg onto her wedge of toast. "Not yet. They haven't filled the police chief's position. Jake Taylor is working as temporary chief. There's no one to make that decision."

"I remember him. He was the desk sergeant. He must be close to fifty. Why haven't they offered him the job?"

"Word is he doesn't want it. Something about pensions and shift premiums. He's nearing retirement, so I guess these things matter." She took a bite of her egg and toast combo, suddenly feeling her hunger. She never ate this well when she was alone.

Liam shrugged. "I suppose as long as they have a good man in the position, they can take their time. The mayor and town council would want a good match, especially after what happened with Evans."

George grimaced as she remembered former Police Chief Evans. He hadn't been corrupt, but he had been a dud. He had focused on George as the prime suspect for the drugs theft. In a way, she understood Evans' reasoning. Thankfully, Liam had figured out she was innocent.

She swallowed and said, "What about you? You probably can't talk about your assignment, but was it bad?"

He hung his head as he pushed his breakfast away. His dark, messy hair, longer than it had been in June, fell over his face as he was thinking. Finally, he straightened. "All I can say is that your father's network has been dissolved. No one will be coming after you, your mom, or sister. You're safe."

If she hadn't been already sitting down, she might have collapsed. She'd never been free of her father. He had no conscience and had thought nothing of starving and torturing his wife and daughters. He was her bogeyman. But she had to wonder what price Liam had paid for her freedom. With his long hair and sunken eyes, he was a shell of the person she'd known just a few short months ago.

"Thanks. But this cost you." Her throat felt thick, and she blinked back hot tears.

He blew out a long breath that ruffled the lock that hung over his eyes. "I was burning out before I came to Magpie. I'm done with undercover work, and I'm not sure about my future with the RCMP." He stared blankly into the distance.

"Is there anything I can do?" Even as she said the words, she knew there wasn't. He needed to figure out his future for himself.

He shook his head. "I'm on leave for the next two weeks. Maybe I'll know what I want to do once it's up."

"Do you have vacation plans?"

"I was hoping I could stay here with you." He gave her a genuine, lopsided grin that made her heart do a little flip.

"Of course." She was suddenly restless. Thinking about her feelings and talking about her life and lack of future had her on edge. "Do you want to get out of the house? I normally go to the Jumping Bean in the morning."

He leaned back in his chair so only two of the four legs were resting on the ground. "You have a routine?"

She picked up her plate and took it to the sink. "I normally workout first thing then head to the coffee shop. I spar with Alan Hammond after lunch." Alan was a fellow officer with the Magpie Police Service. They hadn't always gotten along but, lately, they'd become friends. Her animosity toward him was born out of his reluctance to do paperwork, but he had proven himself to be an upstanding officer when he, and his partner Greg, had stood up for her in the face of former Chief Evans' bias.

"You spar? Is that safe, given...?" He pointed to her head.

She took that to mean her injury. "I wear a helmet. We mainly practice holds, moves, a bit a jujitsu, anything that'll come in handy when restraining a suspect. Alan and I have an agreement —no head punches."

"Good to know." He lifted a single eyebrow as if he found her assurance suspect. He obviously wasn't happy about her practice fights but, thankfully, he had the good sense not to say anything.

"Dibs on the shower," she called and laughed as she made a

dash for the bathroom. Maybe a good host would've allowed him to go first, but there was no way she could coddle him for two weeks. It simply wasn't in her nature, so he might as well get used to it.

CHAPTER THREE

George enjoyed the ride to the Jumping Bean coffee shop in Liam's big Dodge Ram. It was a lot faster than the bright blue bike she'd borrowed from her childhood friend, Andrew McKenzie, who everyone called Buddy.

The smell and feel of soft leather seats were luxurious. She'd only ever owned old beat-up cars. Her Subaru had torn cloth seats, which she'd covered with black polyester, washable seat protectors. The cup holders, which should have been attached to the dashboard, had broken off before she'd purchased it. Her drive to work had always involved wedging a hot cup of coffee between her thighs and hoping it wouldn't spill.

"I see the Rockin Horse is closed," he said as they drove past the bar. The owner, Mattie, had murdered Smokey and attempted to kill George. Mattie was now in prison, awaiting trial for murder. Her son was also in jail for robbing an armored car. A large For Sale banner hung from the faded wood siding.

A pair of magpies swooped in front of them. The old English superstition sprang to mind.

One for sorrow
Two for joy
Three for a girl
Four for a boy
Five for Silver
Six for gold
Seven for a secret never to be told.

For years, George had hated magpies because her mother, Tina, had believed the rhyme as if it were a fact. But lately, George had grown to appreciate the birds as hardy survivors. It was something they had in common.

Liam held her hand as they walked from his truck to the coffee shop. They entered the café just as the seniors' walking group were finishing their drinks. The women smiled and waved at her. Some of them called out her name.

George waved back, happy to see them.

"You weren't as familiar with the locals last time I was here," Liam said as they joined the line to order coffee.

"I knew them, but I worked and didn't frequent the Jumping Bean, so I didn't see them as much. Actually, I have them to thank for inspiring me to create my routine. They walk for an hour and then sit and drink coffee for an hour or two. It fills their morning and gets them out of the house. I decided to do the same, except I work out at the gym first."

The owner, Olivia, was as stylish as ever. Her straight gray shoulder-length hair sported a layered cut that accentuated her oval face. She wore a pair of white pants and a tunic-length light blue top that flowed about her. Despite the hectic pace of her work, she seemed calm and in control, something George envied.

Olivia wrote down the order for the man ahead of them. When she looked up from the till, she gasped as she recognized Liam. "You came back." Ignoring her customer who was trying to pass her a twenty-dollar bill, she ran around the counter and gave Liam a hug and a peck on the cheek.

He seemed to take Olivia's show of affection in his stride. A few months ago, George would've found the older woman's reaction astonishing. Back then, she'd thought Olivia was a stuck-up snob. It had taken her own near-death experience to discover that her new friend was warm-hearted, kind, outspoken, and a little wild.

"How long are you staying?" Olivia asked Liam.

He shrugged. "I'm on leave for two weeks."

"I expect to see you again while you're here," Olivia pronounced. "The pair of you can come to a barbeque at our house. John and I would love to see you." Olivia's husband, John, was the mayor. George had learned he was a man who loved life and wanted everyone around him to be happy.

Liam beamed down at her. "That sounds great."

George smiled and said nothing. It was kind of Olivia to offer, but the idea of attending a social gathering made her nervous. She inwardly recoiled at her own wariness. She could not stay isolated forever. Her life was changing, and she needed to open herself up to new experiences.

Olivia scurried back to her station at the till. "It's settled then." She grabbed the cash from her customer, who then went to sit at a table.

George ordered a mocha frappé and was surprised when Liam ordered a vanilla frappé. She'd always imagined he was a no-nonsense black coffee kind of guy. They waited for their drinks and then sat outside on the deck where they had a view of the lake. The sun shone high in the sky. It was going to be a beautiful late August day. The tourists that normally flocked to Magpie in the summer season had thinned a little. School would be starting in September, less than two weeks away. There was a feeling in the air. Maybe it was the quality of the light, or the faint chill in the breeze, or perhaps it was the fact that the poplar trees had started to turn yellow. Summer was fading into fall. In this part of Alberta, autumn could last anywhere from a month to six weeks. It normally snowed before Halloween. The white stuff wouldn't necessarily stay around in October, but after that, it wouldn't take long before the below freezing temperatures of winter became a regular fixture.

"What's wrong?" Liam asked. "You're frowning."

"I need to give my landlord notice. I've been putting it off," George admitted.

He focused his dark-eyed gaze on her. "Because you can't drive."

"Yes. It's been two months since I had my seizure. If I don't have another one in the next four months, I can get my license back."

"Wait four months and see."

"That might not be a good idea. I'm not sure about riding my bike when the mercury drops to minus forty." Water froze at zero degrees and boiled at a hundred degrees. Temperatures in this part of Alberta varied from minus forty in the winter to plus thirty in the summer. That seventy-degree swing could make life interesting.

He raised an eyebrow. "I see what you mean."

13

"On ice," she added, although he probably didn't need the clarification.

He grimaced. "Where will you go?"

"I don't know. I could move into town and rent a studio on the other side of the highway." She hated the idea of living in an apartment building with a hundred other residents. She was used to having her space.

"They're nice, but will you miss your surroundings, the trees and the lake?"

"And the deer walking across my lawn. Yes, that's one of the reasons I've been putting it off."

"And the other reasons?"

"I don't know what I'm going to do for work once my sick leave runs out."

"Maybe you should just stay put. Everything's up in the air right now for both of us..." He trailed off as he stared into the distance.

She didn't interrupt. She wanted him to fill the silence with his thoughts and feelings.

Finally, he sighed. "I really don't want to go back to the RCMP. I gave Mia, Sergeant Olsen, my resignation. She wouldn't take it. She told me to take some time off and think about it."

"If you don't want to go back, you don't have to. It's your life. You get to choose."

"Thanks." He gave her a startlingly brilliant smile, which made butterflies dance in her stomach.

"Hey, George, aren't you going to introduce me?" Her sister, Grace, appeared on the deck. Her blond hair was swept back in a ponytail. She wore leggings and a designer tank top that accentuated her perfect figure. She was the type of woman who always looked put together, which would've been irritating if Grace wasn't so kind.

She dragged a chair over to their table. "When you weren't home, I figured you'd be here."

George waved her hand toward Liam. "Liam, this is my sister, Grace. Grace this is Liam."

Liam smiled. "It's good to meet you."

Grace grinned. "You, too. Are you back in town long?"

George was grateful she hadn't asked him what his intentions were, but figured it was coming sometime in the future.

"Actually, we were just discussing that. My plans are up in the air. I need some time to figure things out."

"What kind of things?" Grace placed her elbow on the table and supported her chin with her palm, fixed solely on Liam.

Liam met her gaze, not backing down. "Work things."

Grace narrowed her eyes. "When will you decide?"

"I don't know, but I'm relying on Georgina's input. She will be the first to know." Liam held his ground.

George tapped her sister's shoulder to get her attention. "Are you done embarrassing me?"

Grace straightened away from the table and shrugged. "For now. I'm sure I'll figure out new ways to embarrass you in the future."

"What are you doing here on a Thursday? Why aren't you at work?" George asked. Grace owned a successful chain of hair salons, which kept her busy.

"I took the day off to get a tattoo." Grace held out her arm and lifted a bandage to reveal the words Love all, trust a few, do wrong to none. They were etched onto the inside of her right wrist in stylish cursive letters. The skin around the tattoo was raised and red. It looked sore.

"Was it painful?" George asked.

"Yes, so much. I don't know how people get their whole body tattooed."

"Getting inked hurts like a bugger," Liam added.

George tilted her head and narrowed her eyes. "You have a tattoo?"

"Yeah, a Celtic knot on my left shoulder blade."

She didn't remember seeing a tattoo when they'd slept together in June, but then her focus hadn't been on his shoulder blade. "Is it new?"

His eyes widened. "I've had it for about twelve years. I got it before I became a cop. You must've seen it."

15

Grace laughed and then said, "She was distracted."

George could feel her cheeks burning. "I was not." She didn't sound convincing, even to herself.

Grace stifled a giggle. "I have to go and get something to drink." She stood and dashed inside.

Through the open door, George could hear Olivia's loud shrieks of laughter.

She tugged at the hem of her light gray T-shirt. "They're laughing at me because I didn't know you had a tattoo." That wasn't really true. They were mocking her because she'd been so preoccupied with sex that she hadn't really looked at him. She was a cop. She was supposed to pay attention.

Liam leaned forward and gave her a light peck on her lips. "We had more important things to think about." He waggled his eyebrows.

George's face became even hotter, but this time it wasn't from embarrassment. She brushed a lock of hair away from his face. The circles under his eyes were still puffy with fatigue. He was too exhausted for her to make demands of him, but she yearned to trace the lines around his mouth and run her fingertips down his body. "I would love to be that distracted again, but if I'm being too push—"

"Let's go." He grabbed her hand and dragged her toward his truck.

CHAPTER FOUR

Georgina's scent, a mixture of strawberries and cake, was driving Liam crazy. The journey back to her place seemed like the longest of his life. She sat in the passenger seat composed, as if she were going for a job interview. His heart thudded hard in his chest as he thought about her ankles hooked around his waist. *Keep it together, man.*

Finally, he parked in her driveway. Neither of them moved. He was waiting to follow her lead. These days, it was better not to be pushy. He had no idea what she was thinking. She swivelled to face him, her gaze meeting his. Her changeable eyes looked silver now, a stark contrast to her dark hair and her honey-toned complexion. She cleared her throat and then rubbed the frayed hem of her jean shorts. Perhaps she was having second thoughts. She brushed her hair away from her face, revealing her slim neck. He'd read that there were fourteen erogenous zones. The nape was one of them.

God, he wanted to explore her body and give her the pleasure she deserved. But that would only work if she was into it. "Look, if you—"

She pressed her mouth to his. He smothered his surprise, enjoying the feel of her cool lips. He groaned into her mouth as he wrapped his arms around her. He'd dreamed of this for two long, hideous months.

Her hands slid under his shirt to stroke his back. They were hugging across the center console. He would rather they were in bed, but he couldn't seem to stop. He deepened the kiss as her fingertips traced up his spine, making him shiver. Her pointed nipples rubbed against his chest. For a moment, he was too light-headed to react as every nerve ending in his body came alive. He worked his hand under her gray T-shirt, pushed her flimsy bra aside, and strummed her nipple. Her head fell back as she moaned.

His aching penis grew rock hard in response to her uninhibited reaction. He traced small pecks and nips down her neck and then said, "Honey, I want this to be good for you, but I can't do that in this truck."

She gasped for breath as her stunned gazed connected with his. Then a slow smile curved her lips. "Catch me?"

She dashed out of the truck and ran up the steps. He raced after her, enjoying the lightness of the moment. She laughed as she put the key in the lock.

He caught up with her just as the door opened. She squealed with delight when he clasped her around her waist and pinned her against the living room wall.

Her arms wrapped around his neck, her solemn gaze connected with his. "I've missed you."

Her unguarded sincerity was a sucker punch to his chest. She didn't seem capable of playing games. That realization made him wish he could give her the world. Using his index finger, he brushed a long strand of dark hair away from her cheek. "Me, too."

Those inadequate words didn't even begin to describe how he'd felt but, somehow, in the face of her straightforward honesty, he was left speechless.

She tugged him closer so her lips were almost touching his. "Oh, yeah? Prove it."

"Challenge accepted." Using his greater size, he pinned her against the wall with his hips as he ripped her T-shirt over her head and unhooked her bra. She tugged the undergarment off and threw it aside. He sucked a soft pink nipple into his mouth, flicking it with his tongue, and was rewarded when she arched against him.

Her hand rubbed his penis through the fabric of his shorts. His longing, which he'd suppressed for months, couldn't be held back any longer. He lost control.

He attacked her zipper, tugging it down, taking her shorts along with it.

They became a jumble of arms and legs as they tore at each other's clothing. Once his shorts were off, she circled the tip of his engorged penis with her finger, but he batted her hand away.

"Later."

He hoisted her up against the wall, trapping her. "Hook your legs around me."

She did as she was told, her ankles digging into his back. He held her butt, supporting her weight. Then he lowered her slowly, inching her onto him, getting her used to his size, the intrusion. She was tight and so wet it took everything he had not to give into the need to take her fast. Finally, she was embedded to the hilt.

She gasped, panting for breath. "More." The guttural scream tore from her throat.

He obeyed, pounding into her, giving in to the animalistic need to mate with her.

She orgasmed, spasming around him, milking him.

He screamed her name as he joined her, unable to hold back any longer.

"I'm sorry. I couldn't…" He took a break, too winded to talk. "There were things I planned," he panted, struggling to catch his breath. "Do you know there are fourteen erogenous zones?"

She was covered in a layer of sweat, making her damp hair stick to her face and neck. "Fourteen?" she gasped. He was pleased to see she was also out of breath.

He turned and strode across the room, not releasing her.

"Where are you taking me?"

"To bed. I want to explore those zones."

"Good." She buried her face in his neck.

***

Liam lay on his side and ran his index finger along Georgina's spine, enjoying the feel of her. She was firm and muscular, yet soft in all the right places. She smiled but didn't open her eyes. She was relaxed and tired. After they'd made love standing up in the living room, a first for him, they'd moved to the bed where he'd made her come twice, a fact that gave him a certain measure of male satisfaction.

An afternoon in bed with Georgina was a great way to unwind and remind him of what was important.

He flopped onto his back, tucked her against his side, and stared at the ceiling.

"Do you want to talk about it?" she murmured.

"I can't go into details." He hated shutting her out.

"But you can talk about how you feel." Using her fingertip, she traced circles on his abdomen.

There was a long silence. He knew she wouldn't push, not because she didn't care, but because she knew how cases were compartmentalized. No officer talked about an investigation except with those directly involved. But she was right; he could talk about his emotions. "You form relationships when you're undercover. You get to genuinely like some of the people. There was a kid. He wasn't a bad person. His parents were customers and had gotten him a 'job' to help pay for their habit."

The kid had been a weak link, one he had exploited to make the bust. He pictured the boy's face as he watched his parents get arrested.

"And you hope he can find a better life. Is he in danger?" she urged.

"I hope not." He'd made sure the kid was taken away. But he had no control over how angry he would be, or whether or not that rage would turn to hate.

"But it's weighing on you."

"Yeah."

His phone rang, making a distinctive harp sound. "That's my mom's ringtone."

He dashed to the living room and grabbed his shorts off the floor. Then he rummaged through the pockets. He managed to press the button to answer before it went to voicemail. "Hi, Mom."

"J-J-Justin's dead." Her voice had the nasal sound of someone who'd been crying.

"Who's Justin?" He hadn't talked to his parents in months. His father didn't approve of him, which pissed him off. Their mutual animosity meant they had an acrimonious relationship. It was easier on his mom if he kept his distance so she didn't get caught in the middle of their crap.

"He's your dad's assistant. We were downstairs eating dinner, and he was killed," she said and then blew her nose.

"Are you saying this is a homicide?" he asked, deciphering her words.

"Yes. They're still interviewing us."

He could hear the strain in her voice. "Are the police saying anything? Giving you any clue?"

"They think there was a robbery, and Justin interrupted the thief."

"Have the Vancouver police cleared—"

"No, we're in Banff."

"Banff, Alberta?"

"Yes." A sob erupted from her throat.

They were only four hours' drive away. The tourist town was situated in a national park, which meant it came under RCMP jurisdiction. He waited until she stopped crying and then said, "Where are you staying?

"At Derek's house in downtown Banff."

"Derek Sexton?" he asked, clarifying her answer. Sexton was CEO of Starling Stores and his dad's boss.

"It's a business getaway. Derek, your dad, and Justin had informal meetings planned. It had to do with w-w-work." She sounded dazed and confused.

"Do you know what they were discussing?"

"No, it was all very hush-hush. Then Justin died. There was so much blood." Her voice cracked as she broke down and wept, her grief apparent.

He waited for her to gain control again. "Okay, we'll be there by tonight."

"We?" she squeaked and then blew her nose again.

"I'm bringing my girlfriend." He disconnected and then eyed Georgina who stood on the other side of the couch, wearing a robe. Her long dark hair was mussed from their lovemaking. He wished they could go back to bed and spend the rest of the day wrapped in each other's arms, but he couldn't abandon his mom. He tried to smile but wasn't sure if he pulled it off. "Wanna take a trip to Banff?"

"What's going on?" Her tone suggested she'd heard some of the conversation.

"I'm not sure. My dad's assistant was killed in a robbery. My mom sounds pretty shook up." He couldn't remember the last time he'd heard her cry.

"And you want to be there for her."

"Yeah. Will you come with me?"

"Are you sure you want me along? I mean, this is a family thing."

He wanted to tell her she was his family, too, but didn't. It was too soon, and he didn't want to scare her off. "Yes, I'm sure."

She pushed her hair away from her face, not meeting his gaze. "Of course. If you're sure that's what you want." She pursed her lips as if thinking about something. Finally, she said, "You told your mom I was your girlfriend." Her uncertainty and hesitation were palpable.

She was a capable, strong woman, but he suspected she had very little experience with men, and even less practice at relationships. That inexperience had probably made her cautious.

"What if your parents don't like me?" she continued, flopping down on the couch.

He sat beside her and took her hand in his. "I'll be honest. This might be tough for you. Dad can be a jerk. Mom's normally the nice one."

She flinched at his words, her hesitation obvious. "How have they been with your other girlfriends?"

He twisted in his seat to face her. "I haven't introduced any other girlfriends." None of the other women he'd been with had mattered because he hadn't wanted a future with them.

"You haven't?" Her eyes widened with surprise.

He shrugged, trying not to make a big deal out of it. "No. It just never happened. The rift with my dad might have something to do with it. But it would mean a lot to me if you were there."

She released his hand, stood, and paced to the window. He couldn't see her face and had no idea what she was thinking. Then she shrugged. "Well, it's happening now."

He closed the distance between them, turned her to face him, and gave her a quick peck on the lips, trying to reassure her. "And for the record, I think of you as my girlfriend."

She blew out a long breath. "Okay then. I'd better shower and pack." She turned and headed for the bathroom.

CHAPTER FIVE

It was late Friday evening when they arrived in Banff. They'd driven west into the Canadian Rockies and then headed south, enjoying the scenic route. George wouldn't have recommended it in winter. The Icefields Parkway wasn't maintained and was prone to avalanches, but in August it was worth the extra time it took to navigate the peaks and valleys because of the spectacular mountain views. The glaciers were so close it felt as if you could reach out and touch them, and the forests were so vast it seemed as though they went on forever. They'd even spotted a young black bear in a tree by the side of the road.

Banff was a shock to the system after the isolation of their drive. The sidewalks were crowded, and the traffic was reminiscent of rush hour in a major city.

Liam consulted the GPS on his phone and then headed along the main drag. After turning left, they crossed the stone bridge that spanned the Bow River.

Despite the warm evening, her hands were ice-cold. She twisted them together as her heart rate quickened. She'd never met a boyfriend's family before and wasn't expecting a warm reception.

"This is it. Sycamore Street." He turned right.

The house took up the whole block. The south end of the property edged the river. A large red and white sign was pinned to the gray stone wall that surrounded the property, indicating the house was for sale. This had to be prime real estate in town. They pulled up to the wrought iron gates with a pair of deer etched into the metalwork. Liam opened the driver's side window and pressed a button on the security system.

They were buzzed in without announcing themselves which, in George's opinion, defeated the reason for having home protection. But then again, the only safety measure she had at home was a baseball bat, so what did she know?

The gates opened to a circular cement driveway boasting a large brass statute of a moose in the center. An attached three-car garage was situated to the right with the massive house straight ahead. It was built out of the same gray stone as the surrounding wall. Frayed police tape hung from the ornate wood and glass front door. It was the only visible sign that this had been the scene of a crime.

An older woman with short, fair hair rushed through the door. She wore a white tunic-length cotton shirt over a pair of pale blue jeans. Everything about her conveyed good taste and style.

George tugged her T-shirt down over her leggings as she tried to suppress her feelings of inadequacy. She wasn't here to impress his parents. She was here to support Liam, and that was all.

The woman threw herself into Liam's arms. "I'm so glad you're here."

"Hi." Liam squeezed her tight and then untangled himself. "Mom, I'd like you to meet my girlfriend, Georgina. Georgina, this is my mom, Ella."

George held out her hand. "Hi."

"It's nice to meet you." Ella gave her a watery smile but didn't shake her hand. She addressed Liam. "I just wish you were here under better circumstances."

George let her hand fall to her side and tried not to take Ella's snub personally. Liam's mom had graced her with a pleasant smile. Maybe she'd just missed her outstretched hand because she was so upset.

"What happened?" His gaze narrowed as he focused on his mother.

"We were having dinner downstairs when Justin went up to the office to make a call. We were having such a good time we didn't notice he hadn't returned. Finally, your dad went to look for him and found him dead." Ella seemed to slump as she stared into space.

George couldn't tell if she was having trouble coming to terms with the incident or if she was still reeling from the loss, or maybe she was reacting to both.

"That must've been awful," George said, remembering how she'd felt when she'd found her friend Smokey dead two months ago.

Ella sniffed. "It was."

"You said something about a robbery?" Liam threw a hand over George's shoulders and hugged her to his side. She reciprocated by wrapping her arm around his waist.

"We didn't know about that at first. Not until the police told us."

"What was taken?" George asked and then regretted it. This was family business. She should just butt out.

"How do you know something was taken?" A man in his late fifties asked the question as he strolled toward them. If it weren't for his gray receding hair and glasses, he would look like an older version of Liam. He had the same square jaw and brown eyes. He wore cargo shorts with a loose gray dress shirt. A combination that was designed to try to hide his middle-aged belly.

"Georgina, this is my father, William."

William ignored her and addressed Liam. "This is a family matter. You shouldn't have brought a stranger here."

Liam clenched his fists. "She is my family."

George backed out of Liam's grasp. "I don't want to cause any problems. I can stay at a hotel—"

"I'll go with you," Liam announced.

"No," Ella snapped. "Bill, you will behave." She wagged a finger at her husband. "I called Liam and asked him to be here. He's our son."

"And you will both be respectful to Georgina," Liam insisted.

William sighed and nodded. "I apologize. I'm upset about Justin." He seemed more angry than upset, but George kept her mouth shut. Everyone dealt with grief in their own way. Liam had mentioned his dad didn't approve of him or his career choice. Maybe she was caught up in their family drama. If his parents hated his job, there was no way they'd like his cop girlfriend.

"Let's go inside. I'll introduce you to the others." Ella twisted her wedding ring, which struck George as a nervous habit.

There was a small slate-floored foyer where they kicked off their shoes and then entered a large, open room. The floor-to-ceiling windows and the white walls gave the space a light, airy feel. An expensive couch, loveseat, and a pair of armchairs were situated in a large square around a fireplace, which was made of the same gray stone that had been used on the exterior. The floors were a light hardwood. It was the kind of room George had only seen in magazines.

"Derek, this is my son, Liam, and his girlfriend, Georgina." Ella waved a hand in the older man's direction. "This is Derek Sexton. He's the CEO of Starling Stores and is William's boss."

Derek was about the same age as William except he had a full head of white wavy hair and a matching beard. He wore designer jeans and a spotless white T-shirt. He looked soft, but struck George as being deceptively fit. She wouldn't want to underestimate him if he decided to put up a struggle. She inwardly sighed. That was her cop mentality at work. Assessing people on how difficult it would be to arrest them was not something she should be doing in this situation.

Once the introductions were done, Liam pointed to the blade attached to Derek's belt. "That's an interesting knife set."

"You don't need to interrogate him," William snapped.

"Liam, really!" Ella joined her husband's protest.

Liam smiled. "That's the problem with being RCMP. When you ask a question, no one knows if it's idle curiosity or professional interest."

"And which is it?" Derek didn't seem the least bit perturbed by Liam's inquiry.

"It's the former. I've been known to carry a knife, but I've never seen the whistle option. I guess you're a hunter?"

"I don't hunt, but I'm very proud of this purchase." He took the five-inch blade out of its sheath and passed it to Liam. "I do some hiking. Nothing too strenuous, just five kilometers or so."

"Not overnight?" George asked just to be polite. She'd never been camping in her life and had no outdoor survival skills.

"I'm of the age where a comfortable bed is a necessity. I keep this for safety." He held up the whistle. "This incorporates a fire starter into its design, and the blunt end of the hilt can be used as a hammer. I carry it in case I take a fall. God knows, there's no cell service once you get out of town."

Liam handed it back. "That's a nice set." Then he changed the subject. "We're sorry to bust in on you under these difficult circumstances."

Derek grimaced. "Me, too."

"I'm surprised the house isn't still considered a crime scene," Liam stated bluntly.

George would've preferred he be a little more sympathetic, or at least subtle.

Derek shrugged. "It's probably not fair, but one of the perks of being rich and powerful is that I can make a few calls and get the powers-that-be to provide more investigative manpower. That hurried the process along."

Must be nice. George kept her sarcastic comment to herself. She was out of her depth when it came to dealing with the wealthy. Nothing in her experience compared with the opulence she saw before her. The room they were standing in was three times larger than her little home. She couldn't even begin to imagine what the rest of the house was like. "Did they steal much?"

"Just some jewels we had hidden away. It's strange actually. I normally keep them in the safe, but I was in a hurry, so I stowed them in the linen cupboard between the sheets. It's just a fluke the thief found them." Derek paced to the fireplace and stopped with his back to it. "Make yourselves comfortable. My daughter, Andrea, is around here somewhere. Liam, you remember her, don't you?"

"Yes, sir." Liam nodded.

"Please call me Derek. You're not a kid anymore. How's the RCMP suiting you?"

"Fine," Liam snapped, not leaving any room for discussion.

A young woman with perfectly styled, long straight blond hair entered through the kitchen door. Skin-tight leggings and a matching tank were stretched over her perfect size six figure. George guessed her to be in her late-twenties or early-thirties.

"Andrea," Derek called, "come and meet our guests."

Andrea ignored her father, opened the fridge, grabbed a bottle of water, and chugged it down. Then she swiped the back of her hand across her face and turned to them. "Hi." Her eyes were red and swollen, and her face was blotchy. She'd been crying. "I don't mean to be rude, but I need some time alone." She sniffed as she walked past them and ran up the stairs.

Andrea's reaction was a reminder that despite their wealth, these people were suffering a loss, and that was something she could understand.

"Why don't the pair of you take the guest room over the garage. That way you'll have more privacy." Derek smiled, still playing the gracious host and seemingly not the least bit perturbed by his daughter's grief.

"Thanks, but we can stay in a hotel. You guys have a lot going on, and we don't want to be in the way," George said, wanting to put some space between herself and Liam's family. There was an undercurrent between these people. Andrea and Ella seemed genuinely upset. William was obviously angry with Liam, and she couldn't get a read on Derek Sexton, but she'd never trusted charming people.

"It's no trouble. Your room's ready. I'll show you the way," Ella announced in a stern voice. Everything about her demeanour suggested that no one should argue with her.

There was no way George could object without making the situation worse. Liam's gaze snagged hers. It seemed as though he was assessing her, maybe even questioning if she could handle his family. If so, he was right to wonder.

George, Liam, and Ella collected their shoes from the front entrance. Then Ella led them through the kitchen to the back door. From there, they walked across the garden patio, which was an outside entertainment space with a barbeque and what looked like a stone oven. It also boasted a dining area with a long glass-topped table with brass legs, surrounded by eight chairs, which were covered in light green cushions.

"Is this where you were when the robbery occurred?" Liam

asked.

The fact that he hadn't said "homicide," which was the official term for the crime, was not lost on George. She presumed he was trying to protect his mom from the harsh reality of the situation.

"No, it was raining, so we were inside."

At the end of the patio, they turned right into the garage. It smelt of exhaust and oil and housed three sports cars. George recognised the Porsche but couldn't name the other two. They climbed the steps to the second-floor apartment.

The bedroom suite was large, taking up the whole upper floor. It matched the décor she'd seen in the main house, white walls with wooden furniture, high ceilings, and hardwood floors.

There was a king bed near the window at the far end and a big screen TV opposite.

"I'll leave you to get settled." Ella wrung her hands, her tension and hesitation evident.

If George knew Ella a little better, she might have encouraged her to say more, but this was Liam's mom, and she was here to support Liam. Which in this case, meant keeping her mouth shut. "Thanks for everything."

Liam walked to the large picture window and stared out, seemingly transfixed by the view.

From her position by the bed, George could see the river, the street that ran parallel on the other side of the water, and the mountains in the distance. She suspected Liam was more interested in the inhabitants of this house than the scenery.

He turned and strolled across the room to give his mother a hug. "I'm glad you called me."

She sniffed as she nodded and then left without another word.

"Your mom and Andrea seem genuinely upset at Justin's death. I'm not sure about your dad and Sexton."

Liam pursed his lips and made a balancing motion with his hands. "It's hard to get a read on my dad. He might just be angry with me, and it's masking his other emotions. As for Sexton, I haven't seen him in years, not since I was in college. He seems pleasant enough, and from my experience, that's good for a CEO."

"Seriously?"

"I've only met two, both in the course of an investigation, and they were both dickheads."

"Charming." George threw her backpack on the bed and walked to the bathroom. She opened the door to reveal a large ornamental bathtub and a glass-walled shower in the corner. The room was encased in white marble. "This is how you grew up?" she called over her shoulder.

Liam moved to stand behind her. He wrapped his arms around her waist. "We're in the servant's quarters."

She leaned back into him, enjoying the warmth of his embrace. "You're kidding. This room is luxurious."

He shrugged. "Maybe. And for the record, I didn't grow up like this. We were comfortable, but Dad didn't get the job as chief financial officer with Starling Stores until I was twenty. It was a huge step up for him." He straightened away from her and walked back to the bedroom.

She missed the warmth of his touch.

He collapsed onto the king-sized bed. "I'd moved out and was studying at university by the time he got the job."

"Getting your law degree." She bounced onto the mattress and lay on her side, facing him.

He smiled and turned to her. "Yep."

"What does your lawyer's mind tell you about the other guests in this house?"

Using his fingertip, he tucked a strand of hair behind her ear. "No one was pleased to see us."

"Not even your mom? She seemed welcoming enough."

"No, she's hiding something." He lay back and stared at the ceiling. "Something happened between her calling me and us arriving. I just don't know what."

"Why do you say that?" George had sensed a hesitancy in Ella Mason, but she didn't know Liam's mom well enough to make a determination.

"She is the most open person I've ever met. She blurts out her feelings. That normally works in her favor because she always believes the best in people. But now she seems reserved, which, for her, is abnormal. My mom knows more than she's saying."

CHAPTER SIX

They'd woken about thirty minutes before sunrise. At Liam's suggestion, they'd made the most of the shower, which was big enough for two. God, he loved pinning her against a wall. They hadn't yet expanded their lovemaking to include the claw-foot tub, which was how he wanted to spend his day. Unfortunately, that wasn't possible.

Liam held the door open for Georgina as they entered the kitchen. Derek Sexton sat at the kitchen table, reading his tablet. He had a steaming beverage in front of him along with a dish containing a croissant and some strawberries. He pressed a button on the device as they approached, making the screen go blank.

Georgina homed in on the carafe of coffee situated on the counter next to the expensive-looking stainless steel gas range. "May I help myself?" she asked Sexton.

"Of course. There's cream in the fridge and sugar on the table." Sexton smiled, seeming once again like the courteous host, but Liam couldn't shake the feeling that he was watching a play.

He followed Georgina's lead, pouring the dark liquid into his cup. Her cheeks and lips were slightly red from his stubble. She wore jean shorts with a white button-down blouse. Her long, dark hair was still damp from their adventure in the shower.

What the hell was he doing here? He should be back in Magpie, unwinding after his assignment and spending his vacation with Georgina. Instead, he was wasting his time, making small talk with his father's boss.

Maybe he was still operating with his undercover mind. It was the distrustful attitude he employed to help him survive in a covert operation. He hadn't had time to shift his outlook, and this last stint had been particularly grueling.

Or perhaps this skepticism was a result of Georgina's influence. When they'd first met, she'd declared that charm was a veneer people used to disguise who they really were. And Derek was the most charismatic person in this house. Whatever the reason, Liam didn't trust Sexton, but he'd be nice for his parents' sake.

He joined Sexton at the table. "I've never met Justin...Justin... I'm sorry, I can't remember his last name." That was a lie.

"Cross," Sexton supplied. "Justin Cross. He was your dad's assistant."

"What was he like?" Liam asked.

Sexton shrugged. "I didn't know him as well as William, but he seemed efficient, good at his job. He probably would've been promoted in time."

"Was he married?" Georgina joined them, taking the spot next to Liam.

"I'm not sure. I don't even know if he was straight. It's hard to tell these days, and in my position, it's best not to ask. I judge my employees on their ability to do the task at hand. That policy saves me a lot of trouble, and it means that, no matter if they're male, female, gay, straight or whatever, I always have the best person for the job."

She nodded. "I can see how that strategy would work. I just asked because I figured he'd have family who'd need to be notified."

"I left all that to the police. I've contacted Starling Stores Human Resources department. They'll take care of the necessary procedures."

She said nothing, instead taking a sip of her drink. She was probably surprised at the impersonal nature of the corporate world, but Liam wasn't. Sexton wasn't his father's friend. He was his boss, which meant his parents were visiting this house because Sexton had summoned them.

Liam downed his coffee. "Do you mind if we take a look around?"

"Want to see the crime scene, do you?" Sexton picked up a strawberry.

Liam smiled, displaying the charming façade Georgina hated. "Call it professional curiosity."

"Help yourself." He pointed through the living room. "Go up the main stairs and take the first door on the left."

Georgina frowned at Liam, took a long gulp, and then pushed her chair away from the table, following him out of the room.

"What are you thinking?" he asked as they climbed the stairs.

When they reached the office door, she said, "Two things. First, it would've been nice to finish my coffee."

"And second?"

"All this white must show every scuff mark. It would be a pain to clean."

"Scuff marks, really?" He gave her a dead-eyed stare.

She blew him a kiss and graced him with a cheeky grin as they entered a surprisingly small room with a slanted ceiling, telling him the space was squeezed in under the eave of the house.

The only natural light came from a small window, but he would've had to stoop to look out of it because the roof was so low at that point.

A polished wood desk sat in the center of the room with a leather office chair behind it. Two large comfortable chairs, which were covered in pink velvet, were in the middle of the room. A long, thin, pale-varnished table was positioned against the wall on their left.

"I don't see any signs of a struggle," she said, scanning the room. "Although the crime scene techs would've taken away any evidence."

"There isn't much space. If there had been a fight, there'd be more chaos, more stuff out of place." He pointed to the front right corner of the table. The almost black stain was dried blood. "Here, this is where he struck his head."

She grimaced and paled as she stared at the bloody smears on the floor. "He crawled behind the desk. Probably trying to get to a phone to call for help."

"Someone could have grabbed his head and slammed it into the corner," Liam hypothesised.

She turned away, not looking. "That's nasty, and it would take an awful lot of strength, even for a grown man. I don't see that happening, except maybe in movies."

"Okay, so that's out, especially if we assume Justin was relatively young and fit."

"We really can't speculate about this." She backed up until she was standing in the doorway. "We don't know the position of Justin's injury. If he was hit on the forehead, that would present a different scenario than if he was struck on the top of his head. For all we know, he could've tripped and given himself the fatal wound."

"You mean it could've been an accident?" Liam sighed. "I hate that you're making sense. By the way, when were you going to tell me that you don't like the sight of blood?"

She stepped out of the room and crooked her finger, beckoning him to follow her. "I had no idea until I saw it."

"You never came across gory scenes when you were on duty?" He trailed after her, closing the door behind him. He found her assertion hard to believe.

She crossed her arms, covering her chest. "I saw my fair share of bloodied victims, but they were all still alive. I think it's the death that bothers me."

He could understand that. As a cop, when you dealt with victims of violent crime, your focus was on protecting and helping them. You didn't see the blood because you were concentrating on the individual. This scene was all about death.

He pressed her against the wall. "Umm, I'll have to give you something else to think about."

She giggled and, once again, he wished they were back in the shower, or even walking through Banff, visiting all the tourist shops.

Then she placed her hands on his shoulders and pushed, putting some distance between them. "We should keep out of it. You came here because your mom called. You should concentrate on her."

She was right. They could speculate about the crime scene all they wanted, but they weren't part of the investigation and should just butt out.

CHAPTER SEVEN

The morning was one long awkward experience. George didn't know what was worse, dealing with William and Ella's stilted conversation or listening to Liam's attempts to keep the discussion going. The four of them sat on the patio, enduring moments of talk interspersed with long silences.

William seemed to hate them both equally, while Ella was simply quiet and reserved. William's bitterness toward Liam surprised her. It was as though he was so thoroughly disappointed in the man Liam had become, he couldn't bring himself to be civil. Liam had told her that his father disapproved of him becoming a cop. Now that she'd met William, she realized that Liam had understated the situation.

After a long pause, William stood. "I have work to do." He stomped off without saying goodbye.

Ella put her hand over Liam's. "He does care for you in his own way."

Liam kissed her cheek. He stared at his hands for a moment and then bowed his head. Even though George couldn't see the hurt in his eyes, she knew it had to be there. She wished there was something she could say that would make it better, but nothing came to mind.

Ella gave George a weak smile.

Maybe George couldn't do anything about Liam's relationship with his father, but she could give him some time alone with his mom. "I think the pair of you need some space. I'm going to walk into town. It's only a few blocks."

"Are you sure?" Liam asked. He didn't seem to want her to leave, but Ella gave her a grateful smile.

"Sitting in a café, sipping a cup of coffee, is just what I need. I'll do some reading. This is my first visit to Banff. It'll be fun to explore." She didn't add that she needed a break after the stressful morning. Liam had only been back for two days, and they were already thrust into the middle of a family crisis. It wasn't his fault, but it was taking its toll on her. She was used to spending a lot of time alone, and she needed to clear her head.

Liam turned to his mom. "Georgina is what you'd call a coffee addict."

George gave him a sickly-sweet smile. "Everyone needs a hobby."

***

If Magpie was a tourist town, then Banff was a tourist town on steroids. Every inch of the wide sidewalks were packed twenty people deep. The buses, cars, and horse-drawn carriages meant the traffic was congested and slow-moving. Snow-capped mountains surrounded the town, and yet the calm call of nature they offered was not apparent within the few blocks that made up the town, where stores, restaurants, and art galleries catered to visitors from all over the globe.

Most of the architecture was Alpine themed with A-frame roofs, wooden beams, and ornate flowers carved into the wood-work. Other storefronts had a stone and log post design.

As she passed a storefront, an iridescent fossil caught her eye. It was once a prehistoric creature with a circular shell. Now it sat in a jewelry store window, a striking display of rainbow colours.

A woman's slightly nasal voice announced, "That's ammolite. It's a gemstone created from the fossilized remains of an ammonite. The gem is only found in the Bearpaw formation, which stretches from the eastern Rockies into Alberta, Saskatchewan, and Montana."

George turned to see Andrea looking over her shoulder. She wore a long black cotton sundress that was simple and chic in its design. It probably cost more than all of George's clothes combined. The outfit was finished with a shiny black purse that boasted a bamboo handle, a solid gold clasp, and a matching gold chain shoulder strap. A large pair of sunglasses hid her eyes, which suggested to George they were probably red from crying.

"Hi. How are you feeling today?" George smiled.

She sniffed. "As well as can be expected. I think that's the phrase. Daddy was hovering so I had to get out of the house."

"He cares about you." George made her observation a statement, but she honestly couldn't imagine Derek Sexton hovering. But then again, she'd only met him yesterday so there was probably a lot she didn't know about him.

"Walk with me." Andrea looped her arm through George's and started walking along the packed street. "Tell me about you and Liam."

George allowed herself to be swept along, mainly because she didn't want to hurt Andrea's feelings. "There's not much to tell." George was uncomfortable talking about her relationship with Liam. It was all too new. "I'm the girlfriend. I'm just here to support him."

"Ella is lucky to have family who'll come when she calls." There was a hint of resentment in Andrea's voice.

"Don't you have anywhere you can go?" It might help if she had an escape, somewhere she could go to get away from the house where Justin had died.

"No, it's just me and Daddy. Mom left when I was ten. I haven't seen her since. You probably have one of those tight-knit families."

"Not exactly," George hedged. She was curious about Andrea's life. "You and your dad must be close if it's just the two of you."

She shrugged, the movement making her bangles jangle. "I guess. I'm an interior decorator. I worked on rebranding the stores. That's how I met Justin." Her voice cracked a little. "He was very sweet and kind to me." Andrea's tone suggested that she didn't have many caring people in her life, and that Justin's behavior had been the exception.

"Are you still working at the stores?" Talking about her work situation seemed safer than any other subject that came to mind.

"Daddy has put up the funds for me to start my staging business."

"Staging?" George had no idea what that could be.

"When someone wants to sell their home, I help them present it in the best possible light. I mostly tell them to declutter, and then I arrange furniture in a way that sells. It's a gift." She cast her free arm wide as if announcing her talent to the crowded sidewalk.

"I'll bet." George pictured her own untidy home. "Where are we going?"

"To get our nails done. It will make us feel better."

George tugged her arm out of Andrea's grasp. "I'm sorry, I have to meet Liam. She waved her arm in the opposite direction, vaguely conveying a destination. She hated lying, but there was no way she was going to waste an afternoon in Banff sitting in a salon. "Enjoy your manicure."

"I will." Andrea smiled. It seemed like a genuine response, but it was hard for George to tell because her dark glasses hid her eyes.

George waved as she turned and headed back toward the bridge. After walking a few hundred yards in the heat, she gave up on the idea of sitting in an air-conditioned café. There was no way she'd find a seat. She waited in a long line at a coffee shop, grabbed a frappé to go, and backtracked along the main drag.

She finally found a park by the Bow River and, once there, sat in an open area under the shade of a tall fir, enjoying the feel of the cool grass on the hot day.

She watched the traffic moving over the stone bridge. She'd checked a map before she'd left. The road on the other side of the water forked. If she turned to the left, she would eventually come to the iconic Banff Springs Hotel. By all accounts, it was a majestic landmark resort, a castle nestled in the mountains.

If she turned to the right, she could visit the hot spring, which was said to have healing properties. She'd read that the presence of the spring had initiated the growth in the area. She took another sip of her frappé, wondering if she wanted to explore any of it. Maybe she'd just stay here and relax.

She took out her phone and Googled reported robberies in the area. There had been three, including the house they were staying in. Then she did a search for the addresses, wondering if there was any reason these locations had been selected. All of them were for sale, and each internet realty listing showed a detailed floorplan with photos. There couldn't have been a better blueprint for a would-be robber.

"Hey, that looks good. Where'd you get it?"

She glanced up to find a medium-built man with messy, sandy hair and a beard to match, standing in front of her. He was fit looking, perhaps into martial arts, or maybe a gymnast. He pointed to her drink.

She'd been so engrossed in her research she hadn't seen him approach. "Coffee shop a few blocks down." She waved her hand in the general direction.

"Mind if I join you?" He sat, not waiting for her reply.

She said nothing. He obviously didn't care about her answer.

"Are you in town long?" He smiled, but it struck her as phony.

"I have no idea." It was an evasive answer, but there was no reason to tell this stranger anything.

"I'm a reporter, Jeff Davis. I work for Private Source News." He offered her a business card.

She didn't take it. "I've heard of you. Weren't you the one who exposed that politician who was taking kickbacks?"

"Some of my best work." He gave her a self-satisfied smile. If he could've patted his own back, he would have.

"What do you want?" she said, being blunt. There was no way this was a random meeting. This man was making contact with her for a reason.

"What can you tell me about the robbery and death on Sycamore Street?"

"Nothing."

He narrowed his eyes. "Your boyfriend's RCMP."

How the hell did he know that? "So."

"He must know something." His beady-eyed gaze grew hard. His charming demeanour from earlier was gone. This conversation was now an interrogation.

"He's here as a private citizen to support his family. He's not involved in the enquiry, and I'm here to support him." She made sure her tone was unyielding. Given a chance, Davis would run roughshod over her.

"But—"

"If you know anything about the investigative process, you'll know that the detectives in charge of a case do not discuss it with anyone. Even if he asked, which he hasn't, they wouldn't tell him anything."

She paused and then said, "I have a question for you. How do you know about me and my boyfriend?" She wasn't about to mention Liam by name. For all she knew, Davis could've been watching the house and just decided to follow her, thinking she'd be an easy target.

"Your name is Georgina Scott. Your boyfriend is Liam Mason. You're a cop who is on medical leave after an incident where you were knocked out by a drunk. As I said, Mr. Mason is RCMP. My contacts couldn't find out much about his service record."

George stared at him for a minute and then recovered. "You must have some good sources."

"I do." He grinned, revealing his arrogance.

George didn't consider herself a violent woman, but she would love to punch the smug expression off his face. She rubbed her hands along the grass, hoping the coolness would ground her. Finally, she said. "Then I should ask you, what do you know about the robbery and Justin Cross' death?"

He held a red and gold memory stick in one hand, which he flicked with the tip of his thumb. His lips trembled. He inhaled, gathering his self-control. "Nothing really, except the burglar didn't kill him."

Her question had thrown him off. Either he hadn't been expecting it or he hadn't been able to keep his response devoid of emotion.

He stood and walked away without saying goodbye, having said all he had to say.

She didn't chase after him. She knew who he was and where he worked. She'd let the RCMP track him down.

CHAPTER EIGHT

George entered the house on Sycamore Street without being seen. She simply walked through the gates and headed for the garage apartment. She was surprised at the lax security, especially considering one of the guests had been murdered only three days ago.

She'd waited until seven to return in hopes she wouldn't have to interact with any of the other residents. Liam had texted her several times, offering to join her. She suspected that he, too, wanted to escape his parents, but she'd refused.

She lay on the bed and messaged him, letting him know of her return.

He thudded up the stairs two at a time, within minutes of her text, and burst through the door. "I was just about to come and find you and drag you back." He waggled his eyebrows, letting her know he wasn't serious about the "dragging" part. "Did you enjoy your afternoon?"

"It wasn't as relaxing as I thought it would be." She told him about her encounter with the journalist, Jeff Davis.

"I'm surprised you didn't force him to go to the police." He sat next to her.

"I think my days wrestling with suspects are over." She didn't want to think about what that meant for her future. "I figured I'd let the RCMP track him down. We're not involved with the case anyway." She sat and removed a cheap cream sundress from her backpack. She'd wear it to dinner with her jean jacket. It probably wasn't the kind of fancy, designer clothing these people were used to, but she'd only packed leggings, a pair of jean shorts, and three extra-large T-shirts.

"I'm planning to talk to the RCMP tomorrow." His dark eyes assessed her, as though waiting for her response.

She stopped rubbing the creases from her dress. "What really got me was how much he knew about us. I'm telling you, this guy has someone feeding him information."

"You think he has a source in the police?" He put an arm over her shoulder and lay down, pulling her with him so she was tucked into his side.

"At the very least. He knew all about me. He also knew you were RCMP but couldn't find out much about your work."

"He admitted that?" His voice rose.

"Yep, he was that bold, and smug, too."

"I'll add him to my report tomorrow." He pivoted to a sitting position, forcing her to sit too. "We have to get ready for dinner."

She grabbed her dress and headed for the bathroom. "I'll freshen up."

After a quick shower, she took the time to do her hair. Grace had given her a fancy clip that was so easy to use that even she could do it. She dabbed on some mascara and lip gloss, the only makeup she possessed. Both had been a present from her sister. Normally she didn't bother with cosmetics, but she needed the boost. She was out of her depth with Liam's family. She'd be happy if she got through dinner without embarrassing herself or Liam.

She exited the bathroom to find him standing by the door, waiting.

He gave a low whistle. "You look beautiful."

He looked as sexy as ever in a pair of chinos and a white button-down shirt. He led the way downstairs, heading toward the main house. "I apologize for this trip, and my parents."

She slipped her arm through his as they walked across the patio. "Your mom's been fine. Besides, they just want what's best for you."

He stopped and cupped her face. "You're what's best for me."

His lips touched hers. She wrapped her hands around his neck, running her fingers through his soft hair, and tugged him closer, deepening their embrace. Her tongue twined with his, and every inch of her came alive as his hands spanned her waist.

He broke the kiss and rested his forehead against hers. "Come on. Let's get this over with."

They walked through the kitchen door hand in hand to find a buffet of Chinese food in takeout cartons laid out on the kitchen table.

Andrea graced them with a watery smile as they entered. Her eyes were red and swollen, a sign that she was still devastated by Justin's death. "Grab a plate and help yourself. We're sitting in the dining room." Her voice was still gruff and nasally. Obviously, Andrea's manicure had failed to lift her spirits.

The dining table was huge by George's standards, seating sixteen. Thankfully, everyone was squashed at one end. She waited until Liam sat and then positioned herself next to him.

The conversation centered around the weather, the traffic in Banff, and when the ski season would start. George had chosen some beef and broccoli with egg-fried rice. It was delicious, but she found she didn't have much of an appetite. Despite the mundane conversation, she felt a tension in the room, and her encounter with Jeff Davis had left her on edge.

Finally, the discussion faded into silence.

"I can't believe Justin's gone." Andrea blinked back tears.

"How come no one noticed he was absent?" Liam threw the question out there, probably knowing he was setting off a verbal hand grenade.

Ella and William gasped. Derek raised his eyebrows, seemingly curious, and Andrea stared at her plate, pushing her food around with her fork.

Liam's question highlighted a fundamental difference between them. she was just a community cop, who helped people in their daily lives. Whereas he hunted the bad guys for a living, which explained why he was driven to examine the events that led to Justin's death. If Davis was right, and the burglar didn't kill Justin, then someone in this house knew more than they were telling.

William shrugged. "We were all at dinner when he said he had some work to finish up and it would take about thirty minutes. We weren't watching the clock."

"I'm surprised no one heard the robber, given you were all here at the table," Liam pushed.

Ella squirmed in her seat. "That's not strictly true. I left to go find Andy."

"Who's Andy?" Liam asked.

She rolled her eyes. "He's the caterer." Her patronising manner suggested it was normal to be served dinner.

"Did you find him?" Liam persisted.

With the palm of her hand, Ella smoothed her cloth napkin. "Eventually. He was on the patio, smoking a joint. I gave him a talking to. I know it's legal, but he was at work. It's very unprofessional."

"How long were you looking for him?" Liam was like a dog playing tug of war. He wouldn't let it go.

"About ten minutes." Ella played with the edge of the napkin.

"And everyone else?" Liam surveyed the other guests.

Andrea shrugged. "I was here all the time except when I went to the bathroom."

"How long did that take?" Liam countered.

"I was in there a while." She blushed as she pursed her lips, as if deciding how much to share. "There was a lot of cheese in the lasagna, and it upset my stomach." She patted her flat waist. "I'm lactose intolerant. Normally, I pop a pill before a meal and I'm fine, but I forgot."

"What did you think of Justin?" George asked. Of all the people in the house, Andrea seemed the most grief-stricken by his death. Although, in George's experience, men tended to hide their feelings, so it was hard to tell.

Andrea's lips trembled. "I didn't know him very well, but he was always nice to me."

"He was a great assistant but a damn womanizer," William said. "He was married and still flirted with every woman he met."

"I feel sorry for his wife. Luckily, they didn't have any kids," Ella added. "He wasn't even discreet. I heard his marriage was on the rocks."

George focused on Ella. "Is that why his wife didn't join him on this trip?"

"She was invited," William answered for his wife. "I pushed

46

him on it, but he said she wouldn't have a good time and it was better if she didn't come."

"But at work...?" Liam left most of the question unsaid, seeming to want his father to fill in the blanks.

"He was brilliant," William admitted, falling into Liam's trap. "The best assistant I've ever had. He will be impossible to replace. He had a fantastic future in front of him." William sighed, maybe just now realizing what he'd lost.

Liam nodded. "To recap, Mom and Andrea left the table. Dad, did you—?"

"Derek and I were here the whole time until I left to find Justin," William snapped, his patience with his son's questioning spent.

Derek had been watching everyone at the table and hadn't said a word during the whole exchange. He didn't now either, not even to confirm his own alibi.

George wasn't a master at reading body language, but even she knew something was off.

No one was eating, herself included. They all seemed uncomfortable to some degree. Andrea was playing with her food. Derek sat back with his arms crossed, enjoying the show. Ella continued to fold, smooth, and unfold her napkin, and William stared at his plate as though it was the most interesting thing in the world.

"Maybe Andy, the caterer, could've slipped upstairs?" George stated, giving them all an out. Then another thought occurred to her. "But that doesn't explain why no one heard a struggle."

"A struggle?" Derek snapped, turning his intense gaze on her, dropping his jovial host routine.

George shrugged. "It's simple really. If he disturbed a burglar, a stranger, the chances are he would've made a noise, and this room is close enough that you would've heard it."

They all stared at her as the enormity of what she'd said sunk in. If the thief didn't kill Justin, then one of them did. Jeff Davis had been right when he'd suggested there were two separate crimes. Someone had robbed the place, but someone sitting at this table had killed Justin.

CHAPTER NINE

George sipped her coffee and grimaced. She'd added a healthy dose of cream and an unhealthy amount of sugar, but it still tasted like burnt oil.

Liam slumped into the kitchen chair next to her. She knew he hadn't slept well. He'd tossed and turned all night. He looked the same as he had three days ago when he'd shown up at her door. His eyes were puffy, the lines around his mouth seemed deeper, and there was a seriousness to the set of his jaw. She wished she could lighten his load, but that was impossible. His parents were implicated in a homicide, and it was wearing on him.

"Davis was right, wasn't he?" George said, breaking the silence,

"What do you mean?" He took a sip, then stuck out his tongue and made a yuck face. He didn't like the coffee either.

"I guess the fact that no one heard anything has me wondering if the thief stole the jewels and never even knew Justin was dead. Maybe it was just bad timing on his part."

"Who killed Justin then?" Liam rubbed his eyes, his exhaustion apparent.

"Could it have been an accident? People do trip and fall. It happens." George took another sip but immediately regretted it as the burnt sludge trickled down her throat.

Liam was about to reply but snapped his mouth shut when Andrea strolled in.

"Good morning. Liam, do you remember when we went to Harrison Hot Springs?" She poured herself a coffee. "Where's the sugar?" She made a show of looking around. "There it is."

She shimmied over to the table, stood opposite Liam, and then bent so he was staring down the cleavage of her low-cut top.

Liam's gaze connected with George's. His eyes widened, silently questioning Andrea's actions.

He squeezed George's hand, ignoring Andrea's questions. "I'm going to see if I can get in touch with the RCMP officer in charge of the case."

"Do you think they'll tell you anything?" George asked. From the corner of her eye, she saw Andrea unbuttoning her camisole, revealing more of her breasts.

"Probably not, but they might give me an idea of how far along they are in the investigation." He kissed her. It was a light peck, but it sent a message to Andrea who stood on the other side of him.

"I can come with you." Andrea pouted her unnaturally plump lips.

"No, thanks." Liam stood and headed for the door, not looking at her.

George eyed Andrea over her coffee cup as the young woman slumped down in a chair, her right nipple on display. It was pretty bold of her to hit on Liam while George was in the room. No, it wasn't just bold; it was irrational. Since their arrival on Friday evening, Andrea had been pleasant. She had also spent much of her time grieving for Justin Cross, a man who was a married womanizer. So why was she so interested in Liam now? Maybe she was the type of woman who always needed a man's attention, and Liam just happened to be the only age-appropriate man around.

George dug deep, forcing herself to bury her own insecurities. Liam hadn't paid any attention to the woman with her breasts on display. She needed to view the situation logically. Andrea was playing games. She knew from her experience as a cop and the daughter of a drug dealer, there were people who liked to manipulate others. It seemed that Andrea was one of those people. The worst thing George could do was react.

"You know..." Andrea circled the rim of her coffee cup with her right index finger. "This is awkward for me, too. I just don't want to see you get hurt. Liam should never have put you in this position. It was cruel of him."

"Why do you say that?" George walked to the kitchen sink and emptied her mug.

"When he left for his RCMP training, he promised to come back to me. I believe he will. You're just a distraction." Andrea rose, walked through the living room, and headed upstairs.

It was weird that Andrea hadn't mentioned a past with Liam when they'd met in town yesterday. George had no idea if they had a history, but she was sure about one thing—Andrea was toxic with a capital T.

Finding herself alone in the kitchen, she decided to brew another pot of coffee while she thought about Andrea and Liam. She found some grounds in the freezer and then carefully measured the water and added the number of scoops she estimated it would take to make a decent brew. It probably wouldn't be as good as the beans she used at home, but at least it would be drinkable.

She sat down at the table and waited for it to percolate. Although they'd never discussed their past relationships, she knew she wasn't the first woman in Liam's life, just as he wasn't the first man in hers. It was comforting to remember that three days ago Liam had arrived on her doorstep after two months working undercover. She believed he had come back because he wanted to be with her. It was as simple as that. If he wanted to leave, he could. She would never try to track him down. His absence would hurt like hell, but she wouldn't stand in his way. She just needed to have an honest talk with him about Andrea. She wanted the reassurance, if nothing else.

CHAPTER TEN

Liam sat on one side of the metal table, playing solitaire on his phone to pass the time. He'd told the desk sergeant the reason for his visit. Then he'd been led to a gray interview room and told to wait. That had been thirty minutes ago.

Finally, a uniformed officer with white hair entered and gave Liam an appraising look. "I'm Corporal Noah Tremblay."

Liam stood. "Pleased to meet you. Corporal Liam Mason."

Tremblay shook his hand and then said, "Let me be blunt. I called your superior, Sergeant Olsen. She told me to tell you to butt out. You're on leave."

"She's not wrong," Liam said, agreeing with the corporal, who was younger than he seemed. His white hair and pale eyes added ten years to his appearance, but he didn't have any wrinkles, making Liam wonder if Tremblay was an albino.

"So?" Tremblay pointed to the door, silently telling him to leave.

"Look, my mom called me. She's really shaken up by this. I came here to support her, but I'm staying in the house with these people. I'm just here to share what I've heard. If I didn't tell you, Sergeant Olsen would kick my butt."

Tremblay nodded his understanding. "Families are complicated."

Liam sighed. Tremblay's statement was far too accurate for his liking. "The most troubling thing to me is that no one heard anything. If this really was a robbery gone bad, why didn't they hear a struggle?" Liam rubbed a hand over his face, his stubbled jaw reminding him that he hadn't taken the time to shave this morning.

Tremblay frowned. "It's a big house."

"That it is. If they were eating outside, I wouldn't think anything of it, but the office isn't that far from the dining room. They would've heard. Unless of course, Cross just tripped and hit his head."

The corporal said nothing, refusing to share.

Liam couldn't blame him. He would've done the same if he were in Tremblay's position. "It has been suggested that the robbery and homicide might be two separate crimes. And given that no one heard anything, I think they might be right."

"Suggested by whom?" Tremblay growled.

"A reporter named Jeff Davis who works for Private Source News. He approached my girlfriend, Georgina Scott, yesterday."

Tremblay scribbled the name on his notepad. "All avenues are being explored." He then stood and walked out of the room without saying goodbye.

Liam shook his head as he exited the police station. He was out of line to interfere in Tremblay's investigation, and the corporal didn't need his help. The best thing Liam could do was stay out of it.

CHAPTER ELEVEN

George sipped the coffee she'd brewed herself. It wasn't great, but it was so much better than the tar she'd had earlier. Liam had just texted to say he was with the RCMP and would be back soon. She'd wait for him. Maybe they could walk to the Banff Springs Hotel. She could do with the exercise and had always wanted to visit the famous landmark.

She smiled as William marched into the kitchen and sat opposite her. "How much will it cost to make you go away?"

"What?" George hadn't expected William to be friendly, but this was a verbal attack.

"I've done some checking. You're the daughter of a drug dealer."

She inhaled, desperately trying to recover. She couldn't control Liam's parents or what they thought of her. All she could do was contain her own reaction. "That's true." There was no point in denying her past. "I'm also a police officer with the Magpie Police Service."

"Who was investigated for stealing drugs."

"And exonerated." She couldn't keep the outrage out of her voice. If William thought he could use that against her, he was wrong.

"Does Liam know about your past?"

"Yes, he does." Liam was the RCMP officer who'd been sent to investigate her, but she wasn't about to share that detail with his father. "Obviously, your contacts aren't as good as you think. Liam knows everything."

William was aware of way too much for her liking. Perhaps he had the same connections as Jeff Davis, then again maybe not. Magpie was a small town. The events of two months ago were common knowledge. It wouldn't take an investigative genius to make a couple of calls and get all the town gossip.

"You will always hold him back." William's lip turned up in a sneer.

This confrontation wasn't about her past, but about a father's hopes for his son. There was no chance she would ever have a good relationship with her father, but the same couldn't be said of Liam. It had never occurred to her that she would cause a rift in his family. She didn't want to be the reason for their falling-out.

Without a word, she stood and headed for the door.

"I'll pay for your ticket home," William said as she stepped through the doorway.

She stopped but didn't turn to face him. "I will never take a penny from you." She slammed the door after her.

How could that awful man be related to Liam? She stomped up the stairs to the apartment above the garage and flung open the door. The space was just as they'd left it this morning. Liam's tote lay open on the bed. The T-shirt he'd worn yesterday was flung over the handles of his bag. He could remain here if he wanted, but she was done.

If she stayed, she would tell his pompous dad and Liam's slutty ex what she thought of them. She pictured herself kicking William in the balls. There'd be no coming back from that. She grabbed her toothbrush and toiletries out of the bathroom and stuffed them in her backpack. It would be best for everyone if she just left.

CHAPTER TWELVE

Liam entered the house through the front door. He followed the murmurs of conversation coming from the kitchen to find his parents huddled at the table.

"He'll be mad," his mom said.

"It's for the best," his dad replied.

"Who will be mad?" Liam asked.

They both jumped and turned to face him. His mom's face flushed, her cheeks turning bright red. His dad stared at the table, not meeting his gaze.

"Georgina left," Mom admitted.

"What?" What the hell had they done to her?

"I'm sorry." She shook her head. "She would've never fit with our circle. Did you see that cheap dress she wore last night?"

"She looked beautiful. Who cares about the dress?" Liam curled his hands into fists in an attempt to control his rage. How could the pair sitting before him be the same caring people who'd raised him?

"Did you know her father is a drug dealer who's serving time?" Dad took off his glasses and cleaned the lenses with his shirt. An action he employed when he believed he was in the right.

"Of course, I know. Everyone knows. It's not a secret." Liam couldn't believe what he was hearing. "You checked up on her?"

"I made some calls." His dad held his nose in the air as if he was better than Georgina.

"She's not good enough for you. You'll never get ahead tied to a woman like that," his mom reasoned.

"I don't want to get ahead." Liam ground his teeth together, controlling his tone as he suppressed the urge to scream. "How long ago did she leave?"

Neither of them answered as they looked to each other for guidance.

He pounded the table with his fist. "How long ago?"

"Fifteen minutes," his mom admitted.

He stomped to the back door but stopped with his hand on the handle. Even though they'd behaved badly, they were still his parents. He would do what he could to keep them safe. "I'm going after Georgina. We'll be heading back to Magpie. I'm not convinced the burglar killed Justin Cross, and if I'm right, that means someone else did."

"Do you mean one of us killed him?" His dad nodded as if agreeing with Liam, although his words suggested denial. It was an odd reaction but one he'd seen before when questioning suspects. Body language was more honest than words.

Did he believe either of his parents were capable of murder? A couple of days ago he would not have thought it possible, but the people sitting before him were strangers. He'd had his differences with them in the past, but he'd buried them for the sake of the family. He wanted George to be part of his new family, and he wasn't going to let them ruin that. "I need to go. You should leave and go back to Vancouver."

"Don't we have to stay for the investigation?" his mom asked.

"No, you haven't been charged so the police have no right to hamper your movements, but you should call Corporal Tremblay and tell him how to get a hold of you." He closed the door behind him.

He ran up the steps to the garage apartment two at a time. One glance told him Georgina had packed up her things and left. What hurt was the fact that she hadn't even called to tell him she was leaving.

His phone buzzed, playing an upbeat tune he'd programed as Georgina's text tone. It was as though she was reading his mind. She'd sent him her location, the park by the river.

He threw his stuff into his tote and headed her way. He would leave his truck. It had been paid for by his dad, and at this point, he wanted nothing to do with his family's money. He was a grown man, and it was time he acted like it.

He walked a couple of blocks to the park by the Bow River.

Georgina was sitting on the lawn in the shade of a tall pine. Her long legs were stretched out in front of her, and her dark hair hung down over her face as she thumbed her phone.

She glanced up from her screen and then turned back to what she was doing. "Don't try and talk me into staying."

"I won't." He dropped his bag on the ground and then collapsed onto the grass next to her.

She stared at his bag and then gazed at the traffic on the stone bridge. Her expression was unreadable. "You should stay. I don't want to come between you and your family."

"What the fuck did my dad say?" It was impossible to keep the anger out of his voice.

She flinched. "Nothing that wasn't true." She pressed her device. "I can get a shuttle to Calgary airport. From there, I can fly to Edmonton, and then Grace will give me a ride to Magpie."

He put his hand over hers, blocking her view of the phone. "I'm staying with you. It's where I want to be."

She shook her head. "You have a real family."

"So do you."

"My parents…I don't know. We're broken. You're not. You're—"

He almost laughed. "We're no great catch, and my dad is not the upstanding citizen he pretends to be. Let me tell you about the Masons."

She said nothing but tilted her head, her interest apparent.

"I was a spoiled brat. When I was at university, my dad had a real estate firm. I worked for him during my summer break. I discovered some accounting irregularities."

Her silver eyes narrowed. "What kind of irregularities?"

"When people are buying a house, they place a deposit with the realtor to secure the purchase. That money is supposed to go into a trust account for safekeeping."

"And it didn't?"

"No, Dad used it on another deal. No one lost any money, but it was risky. If the sale had fallen through or the other deal had gone belly-up, he would've been in a lot of trouble. That's when I decided I didn't want to be a lawyer. I just don't have the stomach for anything shady. It's not who I want to be. Just because they wear suits and act like they're better than everyone else doesn't mean they are."

"Thanks for telling me." She kissed his cheek.

"I'm sorry about everything," he said.

"It's not your fault your dad offered to pay me to go away."

"He what?"

She hesitated. She didn't seem to want to continue on this path and cause more trouble between him and his parents. "Look, let's just put it behind us. I'm kind of raw from this morning, and I don't want to talk about it right now. Maybe once we're home." She probably knew they'd have to revisit the issue of his parents at some point, especially if their relationship became permanent.

He nodded his agreement. "I've left the truck with my parents. I need to stand on my own two feet, and that means leaving it behind."

She grinned. "I bet that hurt."

He laughed and then said, "You have no idea." He stood and held out his hand to pull her up. "Let's go find a car rental place."

CHAPTER THIRTEEN

The ring road around Calgary was busy for nine on a Sunday night. The lights of the city shone in the distance. The sun had already set, which was another sign that fall was nearly here. George pushed her concerns about her living situation aside, not wanting to think about it again.

It was late by the time they'd left Banff. They'd decided to forgo the scenic route through the Rockies in favor of a more direct one.

They'd had to walk to the Banff Springs Hotel and rent a car from there. The landmark had been everything she dreamed it would be. It wasn't just an opulent hotel. It was an experience. The staff had invited them to explore the grounds and castle while they waited for a vehicle. They'd spent an hour peering in to the four ballrooms, assorted halls, and tea rooms. Gardened terraces overlooked the golf course, forests, and mountain peaks. One wing sported billiard tables for the guests to use, and there was even a bowling alley. Maybe one day, if she saved her money, she'd get to spend a night there.

The rental company only had a compact car available at short notice, which meant every time they drove over a bump, Liam's head hit the roof of the car.

"Tell me about Andrea," George said as they turned north and the city lights faded into the background.

"There's not much to tell. I met her when my dad went to work at Starling Stores, about twelve years ago. Why?"

"She said the two of you used to be an item and you were meant for each other and..." She held up her finger, a silent warning for him not to interrupt. "I'm a distraction and you will go back to her one day."

He gasped and then said, "What?" The dashboard lights provided enough illumination that she could see his eyes were wide with shock.

"That's what she said," George assured him.

"But I've never—"

"Look, you're not my first and I'm not yours, but a little heads-up would've been nice."

"Yeah, and if it ever happens, I'll tell you, but it never happened, not with her. I've never touched her or kissed her. I've never even given her a peck on her damned cheek."

"She came on to you in front of me." Her voice rose, revealing her belated indignation. How she'd managed to suppress it at the time was a mystery.

"I noticed, but I have no idea what that's all about. I'm not her type."

She almost laughed. "Really?" How was that possible? He was smart, handsome, had a great body, and was sexy as hell.

"I'm not rich, and that's something she wants in a man. Maybe even needs from a man. I can't imagine her doing her own housework. It's just not who she is."

George leaned back in her seat. Having seen the house in Banff, she could believe it. Most people wanted to keep their standard of living. That was only natural. Andrea's lifestyle far exceeded hers or Liam's. "That makes sense. Then why did she lie about your past?"

He shook his head. "I have no idea, but I swear on my life, I never had an affair with her."

George decided to let the matter drop. She'd talk it over with Grace and Olivia. It wasn't that she didn't believe Liam. It was just easier to believe the bad stuff. It was what psychologists called negative bias. She'd studied it at university. Her mind was wired to think the bad stuff was true. The fact that William had told her she wasn't good enough for his son didn't help. It all coalesced to make her feel inadequate.

They drove in silence for a few more miles until George said, "I Googled some other robberies in southern Alberta."

A slow smile spread across his face. He was probably relieved by the change in topic. "Did anything interesting pop up?"

"I only looked at crimes that occurred in the last month, and I narrowed the search to upscale houses."

"Which left out the smaller crimes that could be attributed to druggies looking for something to sell for their next fix."

"Exactly. Nearly all of the burglaries happened on properties that were for sale. They had listings on the internet with a detailed floor plan."

"You're kidding?"

"Nope. That means our thief only has to do a quick search from the comfort of their own home."

He frowned. "What about the alarms?"

"The other burglaries also happened when the residents were at home, entertaining guests."

He slapped the steering wheel. "Their security systems would've been turned off. Were they all catered by the same outfit?"

"I don't know, but we should tell the RCMP about it. I made a list of the ones I think are connected. I'll send it to you." She tapped her phone screen, emailing him the list.

"I'll call Mia in the morning and let her contact the relevant people. Dealing with Tremblay was a pain, and we have enough on our plate after the weekend with my parents."

That was an understatement. George felt as if she'd taken an emotional beating, one that wouldn't be easy to overcome. Deep down, she worried that Liam's parents were right. She wasn't good enough for him and never would be.

CHAPTER FOURTEEN

George was awake by sunrise, even though they hadn't arrived home until the early hours of the morning. Liam lay sprawled on his front. She was tempted to trace the Celtic knot on his shoulder but decided against it. She didn't want to wake him.

It was hard to believe she'd missed his tattoo when they'd first slept together two months ago. At the time, she'd been so caught up in her need for him, nothing else had mattered. It was also a reminder that as much as she enjoyed his company, they didn't really know each other. They'd spent two weeks together in June, and for most of that time, he'd been investigating her. It was only now she was learning about his background.

Liam rolled over, taking up the whole bed, effectively pushing her off the edge. His black hair hung over his face, and his jaw was darkened with stubble. She could spend the day watching him sleep, or she could get up and let him rest. He hadn't had a chance to recover. God knows what had happened to him when he'd been undercover, but it had obviously taken a physical and emotional toll.

She crept out of the room, made her way to the bathroom, and jumped in the shower. Then she quickly dressed in a pair of shorts and her favorite black T-shirt with a big pink heart imprinted on the front.

Even though it was early, it was already warm, which meant it would be a hot day. She brushed her hair and left it to dry naturally. There was no point in fussing. Liam had seen her at her worst.

It was strange how she could be so comfortable with him and yet still doubted her worth. Damn, William had really done a number on her. Most of the time, she didn't care what people thought. She couldn't afford to. She was the daughter of a drug dealer. There would always be someone who would throw that in her face. But Liam's parents had found her so wanting they had investigated her and tried to pay her off.

She padded to the kitchen, ground fresh coffee beans, and set the coffee to brew, grateful to be back in her own home. Her house was faded, the floor was a cheap laminate, and the walls could probably do with another coat of paint, but it was home, at least for now. She took her steaming mug out on to the front deck to watch the birds on the lake.

Liam joined her a few minutes later. "Morning," he mumbled, his eyes still puffy with sleep as he flopped into the chair next to her. He wore nothing but a pair of cargo shorts. He took two long swallows of his coffee and then said, "What are your plans today?"

She shrugged. "Nothing really. I might go and see Olivia." She was tempted to stay home and deal with her emotional wounds, but it would be better to talk to a friend.

"You know everything my dad said is a lie." It was as if he'd read her thoughts. "The same goes for Andrea. I don't know what's going on in that house, but I think they attacked you for a reason."

She almost laughed. "What reason would that be?"

He stretched out his long legs, putting his feet on the deck rail. "You said the homicide and the robbery were two separate crimes. After that, you had a bullseye on your butt. They wanted to get rid of you."

"I said they might be two separate crimes. That theory explains your parents' actions but not Andrea's. Besides, I was just repeating what Jeff Davis said."

"Yeah, I know, but given how they reacted, I think you got a little too close to the truth."

"And that means your parents are mixed up in it."

"Agreed. I think they're up to their necks in it." He rolled his shoulders, working out the kinks.

"What are you going to do?"

He stared out at the lake, showing no visible reaction. "Have you heard of red-collar crime?"

"Yes, it's when white-collar crime turns deadly. I read a study about it recently." She subscribed to several police publications. The article was featured in one of them.

He nodded. "Sergeant Olsen made me attend a seminar on it. Red-collar crime happens when people who commit white-collar crime kill to prevent themselves from getting caught."

"Derek Sexton and your dad both work for Starling Stores," she said, pointing out the obvious.

"And Dad has a history of not obeying the rules."

"What are you going to do?" She repeated her earlier question, placing her hand over his, hoping he would understand that she was offering him comfort and support. She couldn't even begin to imagine what he was going through. Her father was a criminal who had abused her, her mom, and her sister. She was happy he was in prison where he belonged. But, by all accounts, William had been there for Liam when he was growing up and had provided a home. They might not have a good relationship as adults, but Liam still cared about his family.

He turned his palm up, threaded his fingers through hers, and squeezed. "I'm still an RCMP member. I have to take my suspicions to my superiors. I was going to call Mia Olsen, anyway, and inform her of your discovery."

"You mean how the burglaries occurred in houses that are for sale? I'm sure they've already made the connection."

"Maybe, but it doesn't hurt to check."

She released his hand and stood. "While you're making your phone call, I'm going to ride into town and visit with Olivia. You can meet me at the Jumping Bean when you're done."

He looked up at her and, once again, she was gut-punched by his exhaustion. The crimes and drama that had unfolded in Banff were the last thing he needed. Families were a pain in the ass, but he was too good a person to ignore them when they were in trouble.

"I'll be a while. I have to return the rental car, and I texted Buddy when I woke up. He said if he's free, he'll look at your Subaru." He graced her with a lopsided grin. "Do you have the keys?"

"Sure." She went inside and found her backpack on the couch. She'd dumped it there when they'd arrived home in the middle of the night. She fished her keyring out of the front pouch and unhooked her car key. "Here you go. It was in working order a couple of months ago, but I haven't touched it since..." She didn't want to say since her seizure. Talking about that was like picking at an open wound.

He eyed her for a moment and then said, "We're quite the pair, aren't we?

"What do you mean?"

"I'm burned out and you're out hurt."

She said nothing. She didn't know whose situation was worse. Hers for being injured at work or his for being sick of work. Maybe it didn't matter. This wasn't a competition. Supporting Liam, helping him, meant she wasn't wallowing which, in turn, helped her cope.

She kissed his cheek, then slung her backpack over her shoulders, unlocked her bike from the deck railing, and gave him a bright smile. "We'll figure it out."

**

Liam sat at the kitchen table with his phone in front of him. He needed to choose his words carefully. As pissed off as he was with his father, he didn't want him to get into trouble. Although, Liam couldn't hide from the implications. His dad's assistant had been killed. His parents had been rude to Georgina. Even his mom had judged her because she hadn't worn designer labels, which was out of character for Ella Mason.

Just thinking about it made his hands clench into fists. They'd hurt Georgina. He'd seen the spark in her eyes fade. The pain of their words had torn her to shreds on the inside. He knew the damage they'd done couldn't easily be repaired. She'd always been strong and fought hard to help the people in her community, but how could she fight against someone who clawed away at her self-worth?

He drummed his fingers on the table, working to push aside his outrage and his emotional connection to the case, just as he did when working undercover.

He dialed Sergeant Mia Olsen's number. She picked up on the

second ring. "Are you still causing trouble?"

"Not by design. We're back in Magpie."

"Good." Her tone was abrupt. He suspected purposely so.

"Do you have time to talk? I need to tell you about a couple of things."

She gave a long sigh. "Go ahead."

He could almost feel her frustration. "You know my girlfriend, Georgina Scott."

"Yes, smart woman. She figured out who was stealing drugs from the Magpie Police Service evidence locker."

"That's right. At dinner on Saturday night, she made an off-hand remark, putting forward Jeff Davis' suggestion that the robbery and the homicide were two separate incidents. I think it was right on the money."

"Why?" She didn't ask about Davis, which meant Corporal Tremblay had kept her informed.

"This isn't evidence…" He hesitated, wondering how to explain an instinct.

"You know how this works. Just tell me who said, and did, what. Let us figure out the how and why." By "us," she meant the RCMP.

He told Mia what Andrea and his parents had said to Georgina. "It just feels as though she was being driven away."

"And you think it's because she was getting too close to the truth?"

"Maybe." Now that he'd said it aloud, he realized how flimsy it all sounded.

"Or maybe your parents are snobs who don't like your girlfriend," Mia reasoned.

"Perhaps you're right. They even knew about her dad."

"Are you saying that your parents did a background check on Georgina?" She didn't attempt to hide her surprise.

"Yes, and they tried to pay her to go away."

She laughed and then said, "And I thought my in-laws were bad."

"There's something else."

"What's that?"

"I'm sending you a list of burglaries. Georgina says they might be connected."

"You know your girlfriend can be wrong."

"You don't have to remind me. She drank poisoned coffee because she trusted an old friend, but I don't believe she's wrong about this." He hung up and rubbed his hand over his face. He had the beginnings of a beard. Damn it, he still hadn't gotten around to shaving. Mia could do what she wanted with the information he'd just given her. It wasn't his problem anymore.

He'd get his chores done and then join Georgina at the Jumping bean.

CHAPTER FIFTEEN

The Jumping Bean was packed when George arrived mid-morning. Olivia waved but didn't stop to talk. She was busy making drinks with an impressive amount of speed and coordination.

George waited for her latte and then stood by the counter, searching for somewhere to sit. She spotted an empty table at the rear of the café by the bathrooms and rushed to take the seat before one of the other patrons claimed it.

Maybe it was just as well Olivia was busy. She'd thought telling Olivia what had happened in Banff would help, but now she wasn't sure she wanted to give a voice to her self-doubt. That would make it more real than just an idea, which could be easily dismissed. Although she knew her insecurities would never be completely banished. Growing up with Hank Scott as a father had seen to that. Until recently, she'd had a purpose, but now everything in her life had changed. Her emotions had undergone the greatest transformation. Her world was in flux, and she was forming relationships, which meant she cared. She was now vulnerable.

Perhaps Liam had been right when he'd said all the trouble in Banff started with her repeating Davis' claim about Justin's death. That was a logical, reasoned argument, but her feelings weren't always rational. Deep down, she believed she wasn't good enough for him.

Liam's parents weren't the first people to throw her family circumstances in her face. Her old boss, Chief Evans, had said much the same thing. It was the reason he'd wrongly focused on her as the person who was stealing drugs from the evidence locker.

She took a long sip of her latte and tried to figure it out. She had no say in how other people perceived her. All she could control was herself and her own behavior. But she wanted Liam's family to like her. As soon as his mom had called to tell him about Justin Cross' death, he had rushed to her side. His actions revealed how much they meant to him.

She stared through the crowd out to the street. She was twisting herself in knots over Liam, and yet they'd made no commitment to each other. For all she knew, he would disappear tomorrow. She didn't really think that would happen. Her gut told her they were on the same wavelength and he wanted to hang around and see where this thing between them went. They hadn't discussed their future, which made sense considering he'd only returned on Thursday and it was now Monday morning.

A man with scruffy fair hair caught her eye as he squeezed between two tables, apologized for disturbing the other patrons, and settled in a seat by the window. What was Jeff Davis from Private Source News doing here? Had he followed them so he could check up on them?

She slung her backpack over her shoulder and inched through the packed café.

Last time they'd met, he'd had her at a disadvantage. This time she would be asking the questions. He was on his phone, which meant he wouldn't be expecting her ambush.

"In two days, this story will be published unless we can come to an arrangement," Davis demanded of the person on the other end of the line.

George stopped. Was he blackmailing someone?

She backtracked to a table occupied by Harry Bawa and his wife and ducked down so it seemed as if she was talking to them. Harry was Buddy's boss and owned the Magpie Marine Repair and Sales. "Hi, how are you?" She was acquainted with the couple and waved hello, but they'd never had a conversation.

Both Harry and his wife stared at her as if she'd lost her mind. Harry's wife, whose name she couldn't remember, wore a turquoise, east-Indian style tunic dress, which complemented her dark coloring.

"Good." Harry gave George an appraising look. "Are you okay? You seem strange."

"I have a caramel frappé for Jeff," Olivia called, too busy to deliver the drink herself.

Davis rose, leaving his stuff at his table, and weaved through the crowded coffee shop to the counter.

"I'm fine. Thanks." George patted the table and stood.

Jeff was busy thanking Olivia. George only had a second to figure out what he was up to. She couldn't take his open laptop or phone. He would notice. A red and gold memory stick stuck out of his computer bag pocket. Could it be the same stick he'd had in Banff? There was only one way to find out. She grabbed it and headed for the door.

Oh, my god. She'd stolen Davis' USB drive. How long did she have before he noticed it was gone?

CHAPTER SIXTEEN

George peddled through the alley that ran along the side of the coffee shop. This was by far the most insane thing she'd ever done. She turned right onto Main Street and rode for one block until she reached the library. With any luck, Davis hadn't noticed the stick was gone.

She took the time to lock her bike, but only because it belonged to her friend, Buddy, and it wasn't hers to lose.

Luckily, the library was quiet.

Elijah Thomas, the librarian, sat behind the front desk, scanning the returned books. His long hair, a testament to his Cree ancestry, was tied back in a neat ponytail. He was probably the most studious man George had ever met. He had a passion for books and learning. She'd known him to read works on astronomy, philosophy, mechanical engineering, and gardening. He just seemed to enjoy absorbing knowledge. Whether he used his expertise for any practical applications, George couldn't say.

"Hey, Elijah, can I use a computer?" The library had six desktop models that members could use free of charge.

"Sure. Take number five."

She sat at the relevant workstation and plugged in the flash drive. Twenty pages of numbers appeared on the screen. She hit print so she would have a copy. They were some kind of bookkeeping records. She kept her bank account in pretty good order, but the data in front of her made no sense whatsoever.

She stopped Elijah as he pushed his cart toward the shelves. "Do you have any books on accounting?"

He rubbed his chin and then said, "Which discipline? We have paperbacks on tax accounting, cost accounting, management accounting, financial accounting, and external auditing."

She gaped at him and shook her head. "I don't know."

He leaned over her shoulder, narrowing his eyes as he peered at the numbers on the screen. Then he straightened and said, "If I were you, I'd show this to John King."

"The mayor? Olivia's husband?"

"Yeah, he's a good accountant. The band council on the reservation employs him to do their taxes."

For some reason, it had never occurred to her to ask John for help, even though she knew about his day job. "Okay. Thanks."

She ejected the USB drive, paid for her copies, and then left the library, heading back to the coffee shop.

CHAPTER SEVENTEEN

George remembered to lock the bike again when she returned to the Jumping Bean.

She entered the coffee shop and made a beeline for Liam, who stood at the counter, sipping his black coffee. "Where were you?"

"You don't want to know." She scanned the café.

Jeff Davis sat in his table by the window. Unfortunately, he recognized her and waved. It would be really hard to return the stolen flash drive while he was looking straight at her. Trying not to panic, she waved back.

Shit. She hadn't wanted Liam to know what she'd done. If he wasn't aware, he couldn't be blamed, but it was too late for that. She would have to come clean. But first things first.

She reached up on tiptoe and whispered in Liam's ear. "I need you to follow my lead. No questions asked."

His eyes widened. "What?"

She slipped her hand in his and yanked him toward the reporter.

"Liam, I'd like you to meet Jeff Davis. He writes for Private Source News. He was in Banff and has an interest in the robbery." She pointed her thumb at Liam. "Jeff, this is Liam Mason, the RCMP member whose record you tried to uncover."

Liam scowled, his hostility evident. "Who is your source in the RCMP? And why are you so interested in a run-of-the-mill robbery?" Liam thumped the table. Either he was unaware or didn't care that he was making a scene.

"I was in the area. And I never divulge my sources." Davis shrugged, seeming nonchalant, but it struck George as an act.

She pretended to peer under his table. "What's...?" Then she reached down and faked picking up the memory stick. Standing tall, she opened her fist to reveal the USB drive lying in the palm of her hand. "Does this belong to you?"

"Yes, thank you. It must've fallen out of my bag." Davis scooped it up and stuffed it in the front pocket of his jeans.

Liam had gone silent. He'd probably seen through her subterfuge and was waiting until they were alone for her to explain.

"What brings you to Magpie?" George made mundane conversation, sounding calm and reasonable after Liam's outburst.

"I was hoping to do a story on you." Davis pointed at her.

"Me?" She couldn't suppress her surprise.

"Yes, I'd like to do an article on you. Drug dealer's daughter becomes a cop and makes good. My editor thinks it'll get a lot of interest."

George shook her head. The last thing she wanted was "interest" in her life. "Absolutely not."

He stood and leaned forward so they were face-to-face, as if challenging her to a fight. "I'm writing the story whether you cooperate or not."

Liam shoved his way between them. "Who have you been talking to? I want your informant," he snapped, demanding the information for a second time.

Davis smirked. "It's like I said, a reporter never reveals his sources."

George glanced around the room. Everyone in the Jumping Bean was staring at them, which was not surprising. This was going to escalate. There was no way Davis was going to tell Liam what he wanted to know, and fighting with the reporter, especially in public, would be counterproductive.

"Oh, look, a free table." George grabbed Liam's elbow and forcibly dragged him across the room to the spot she'd vacated earlier. He must've seen the futility of their situation too, either that or he was just following her lead, because he didn't resist. He was strong enough that if he hadn't wanted to go, she couldn't have forced him.

She threw her backpack on the table and collapsed into the chair. From her position, with the seating area to her left, she could see everything except the counter. She watched as Davis stuffed his laptop into his bag, his movements abrupt and angry.

"What an asshole," Liam spat as he sat opposite her.

George nodded. No matter what, her past was going to follow her. There was no getting away from it. "I don't think there's any way to stop him writing a story about me. And now that I think about it, I don't think it'll be hot news. I'm just not that interesting."

Liam shrugged. "Unless he embellishes the truth."

She hadn't thought of that. "You studied law. Is there anything I can do if he prints lies about me?"

"Off the top of my head, I'd say you could sue him for slander, especially since you've never committed a crime." He narrowed his gaze, propped his elbows on the table, leaned in close, and whispered, "Except for stealing his USB stick."

George flinched. "You saw that?"

"Why?" He mouthed the word, hardly making a sound. But his open mouth and wide eyes conveyed his obvious shock at her actions.

"I heard him on the phone. I think he was blackmailing someone, but I could've been wrong."

"What did he say?" he murmured. His voice still deliberately low.

Matching his tone, George repeated the one-sided conversation she'd heard and the fact that Davis had used the word "arrangement."

"And as you know, I returned it..." She cringed, realizing she would have to admit the truth. "After I printed out the contents."

He slapped the table, laughed, and then said, "That's awesome."

She jumped at his unexpected, loud, and exuberant reaction. "Awesome? I thought you'd be mad."

He shrugged as he once again leaned in. "I've done worse. Besides, I'd like it if my parents could get ahead of this so they can organize their legal defense."

She ignored his comment about his family, concentrating instead on the first part of his statement. "Working undercover?"

His chin dropped to his chest, an obvious sign that he wasn't proud of his past actions.

From the corner of her eye, she saw Davis stand and exit the café, his phone to his ear.

Liam patted her hand to get her attention. "Don't stare."

She gave him a rueful smile. "I'd never make a good undercover cop."

"Any idea what was on the stick?" he asked, bringing her back to the subject at hand.

"They look like accounting records." She pulled a stack of papers from her backpack.

"That makes sense. My dad's the Chief Financial Officer for Starling Stores, and his assistant was murdered. Whatever's going on, my parents are in the middle of it." He tapped the pages in front of him. "We'll have to hand these over to Mia and be upfront about how we got them."

"Won't she be pissed?"

Liam raised an eyebrow. "Royally. But before we get chewed out, let's figure out what they mean."

George fingered the documents. "I can't make them out. Elijah, the librarian, suggested we talk to Olivia's husband."

"The mayor?"

"He's also an accountant. Apparently, he's a good one."

Some of the customers had cleared out, but Olivia was still busy, going from table to table, wiping them down and collecting dirty dishware. George waved her over. "We need to talk to John. Do you know where he is?"

"He's at the townhall. He'll be there for another hour."

Liam held George's hand as they left the café. "Leave your bike. We'll walk."

They strolled through the alley next to the Jumping bean, the same passageway George had frantically ridden through less than an hour ago. The traffic on Main Street was busy for a Monday, something she hadn't noticed earlier.

The Magpie Townhall was a new building, which had only been completed last year. It was constructed of red stone and white stucco with a matching red roof. A landscaped garden, which boasted fountains and a brass life-sized statue of children playing, was situated on the right side, and a parking lot sat on the left.

George almost sighed when they entered the cool air-conditioned interior. The receptionist, a pretty woman with glasses who wore her dark hair pinned in a bun, pointed them in the direction of the mayor's office.

They found John King sitting behind his desk, fighting with his stapler. He was a plain man with thinning brown hair and a slim build, but his eyes sparkled with a merriment that matched his easy smile.

"Can you help us figure out these documents?" George held up the accounts she'd printed off.

The mayor tilted his head. "What are they?"

"We're not sure. We're hoping you can tell us." She placed the papers on his desk.

John glanced at the pages in front of him. "This is highly irregular."

"I could be wrong, but I think someone was murdered over this," George stated. She could be making a huge error. The records on the memory stick might have nothing to do with Cross' death or the robbery at the house in Banff. But the way Davis had been playing with the USB drive when they first met gave her the impression that the information it contained was important. She was betting on a hunch, pure and simple.

"We're going to hand it over to the police, but we just want to know what they mean first," Liam added.

"Murder, you say?" John peered at Liam and then at George over the rim of his glasses. "Here in Magpie?"

"No," George admitted. "It happened in Banff, but the reporter who owns the memory stick that holds these files is here. He was in the Jumping Bean today."

"He's here. In our town." John cleared his throat and then pulled the accounts toward him. "Then we'd better find out what he's up to."

George and Liam paced the room for about thirty minutes while John studied the numbers. Finally, he said, "This is bad, very bad."

"What is?" Liam demanded.

"Someone high up at Starling Stores is stealing the workers' pensions." He shook his head. "Criminal."

"Shit." Liam paled. His hands covered his eyes. He must have assumed that his dad was involved, which meant he could also be responsible for Justin's death.

"You don't know it's him," George said, trying to give Liam hope.

"Do you know the person responsible?" the mayor asked.

George glanced at Liam and then at the mayor. "We think so."

Liam faced her. His Adam's apple bobbed, the pain in his gaze apparent. He turned to stare out the window. "It's like I said. He's the CFO. He has to know about it, whether he's stealing or not."

"That still doesn't mean that he killed Justin."

Liam sighed, fished his phone from his pocket, and then dialed. "Mia, we need to talk. There's something you need to see."

CHAPTER EIGHTEEN

Liam could tell Mia was pissed by the rigid way she held her body. It was as though she had to maintain strict control over her muscles for fear she would lash out. She'd commandeered an interview room at the Magpie Police Station. Despite being a petite blond and a mother to four children, she was a force to be reckoned with. If any officer stepped out of line, she did not hesitate to give them a verbal lashing they would remember.

"You're lucky I was on my way here to warn you two to back off." She slammed her heavy, black purse on the table, reached in, and pulled out a notebook.

"This is my fault," Georgina admitted. "Liam had nothing to do with it."

He appreciated that she was trying to protect him, but there was no need. He'd wanted to see what was on the stick as much as she did.

She'd crossed a line when she'd stolen and copied the USB drive and she knew it, but he'd still walked her to the mayor's office to get the accounts analyzed. The problem was the RCMP wouldn't be able to use the evidence they'd discovered. It was tainted, but it might point them in the right direction.

"We'll get back to that later. Right now, I want the pair of you to tell me what you know, suspect or surmise, or any other half-baked ideas you might have formed in your tiny little minds." She shouted the last sentence.

Oh yeah, she's livid. Liam decided the best way to deal with this was to admit the truth and handle the fallout.

Georgina opened her mouth, but he placed his hand over hers, silently telling her to let him speak. She nodded, acknowledging his request.

"My parents are involved, and I needed to know." He reminded Mia of everything that had happened in Banff and told her about the memory stick, printing the documents, having John King look at them and, lastly, the pension theft.

Mia turned her attention to Georgina. "How do you think Davis got this information?"

Georgina pressed her lips together as she considered the question before she said, "I think you need to question Jeff Davis about his contacts. He had these files on a memory stick, which means he's investigating Starling Stores. He'd checked me out before he approached me in Banff. That suggests he was watching the house. He knew who the players were and what they looked like. He also told me he hadn't been able to find out much about Liam's work with the RCMP. But just the fact that he thought he could find out should be a glaring red flag for you."

Mia took notes, not reacting to Georgina's assertion. She was a seasoned officer who knew that the best way to get information was to let the subject talk.

"Maybe it's just me," Georgina continued, "but I think Davis is the key to this whole thing. She rubbed her hand across the edge of her shorts, smoothing them. "You understand that this is supposition on my part. I don't really know anything."

"In other words, we have no proof," Liam added. "But if Davis hands the USB drive over to you, then it won't matter that we knew about it first."

Mia gave a terse nod of agreement but made no comment on Georgina's conjecture, which wasn't a surprise. She probably realized that any observation on her part would be scrutinized by the pair of them later.

"With your permission, I'd like to call my dad." Liam ignored the sour taste in his mouth and the ache in the pit of his stomach at the thought of his father's connection to pension theft and a homicide.

"Do you think it will help?" Mia asked.

"I need to know what part he played in all of this."

"Okay, but put it on speaker," Mia ordered.

Liam's fingers were numb as he dialed the number. He then placed the phone in the center of the table.

His father answered on the second ring.

"What do you know about stolen pension funds from Starling Stores?" Liam snapped, not giving him any time to think.

"H-h-how do you know about that?" His dad sounded rattled.

"It's my job to know." He hated being a hard-ass but not as much as he detested the idea of his dad going to prison.

"Look, son, I know I've done some shady things in the past, but no one ever lost a penny. Everyone always got their money. Taking someone's pension, their retirement, I would never do that. I may not always be on the up and up, but I'm not an absolute bastard."

"Then how did it happen?" Liam challenged, wanting to keep his dad on the defense and rattled enough, frightened enough, to answer honestly.

The line was silent for so long that Liam thought he wouldn't answer, but finally he said, "You know when I was in real estate, I sometimes used client's deposit money to prop up other projects instead of putting it into a trust fund where it would be safe."

"Yes."

Mia gave him a hard look. He hadn't disclosed that fact to her and, sooner or later, she would want to know why. That kind of corruption within his own family meant he was vulnerable to coercion.

"Derek knew about that, too. He threatened to go to the police unless I transferred the pension funds into his account." The fear in his dad's voice was palpable.

"He needed you to sign off on the transfer because you're the Chief Financial Officer," Liam said, making sure he understood his dad's involvement in the process.

"Y-yes." His dad's nervousness was evident, but he seemed to be holding it together.

"I read about a car manufacture in Ontario who took pension funds to pay their bills," Georgina interrupted. "What you're doing isn't illegal, is it?"

"In that case, the company went bankrupt, so it was perfectly legal." If his dad was surprised to hear her voice, he didn't show it.

"But Starling Stores hasn't declared bankruptcy," Liam clarified.

"No. Sexton made some bad investments. He was stealing money for his personal use." Justin and I decided to go to the press. It was the only way we could stop it. Justin did some online sleuthing and came up with a way to pass off the proof to the press without anyone knowing."

Liam blew out a long breath and then said, "But I guess someone found out—"

"Because he's dead," Georgina supplied.

"This is Sergeant Olsen with the RCMP. Where are you now, Mr. Mason?"

"Liam told us to go home, which is what we did." Mia's presence on the call had shaken him. "I'm at our house in Vancouver. Once Derek and his daughter left Banff, we felt it was okay to do the same."

That last sentence was a telling admission of the hold Derek Sexton had over his parents. His dad was being blackmailed and forced to steal the pension funds from Starling Stores employees, and there was nothing they could do to stop him because Derek knew about his dad's past crimes. Sexton essentially owned his parents.

"Stay where you are," Mia continued. "An RCMP officer will be visiting you shortly. You'll need to make a formal statement. For the record, instead of going to the media, you should have informed us, the RCMP." She reached over to disconnect the call.

"Wait." Liam put a hand out to stop her. "Dad, I need to speak to Mom."

There was a rustling sound. He could hear his dad whispering but couldn't make out what was said.

"Hello." His mom's voice quivered.

Liam could tell by the echo on the line that the phone was now on speaker. "Mom, did it really take you ten minutes to find the caterer...what was his name?"

"Andy," his mom supplied. "No, of course not," she snapped. "We shared a joint. There, now you know."

"Do the pol—"

"Yes, the police know, and your father knows. I just didn't want you to know."

"She reeked of marijuana when she came back to the table," his dad confirmed.

"You'd get high, too, if you had to put up with Derek Sexton and his hideous daughter," she yelled, not even attempting to conceal her anger.

Liam sighed. When they'd arrived at Banff, his mom had claimed she was having such a good time she hadn't noticed Justin's absence. That had been a lie, an innocent one maybe, but it had masked the real relationship between his parents and the Sextons. There were always secrets within a family, not necessarily big secrets, but little ones like his mom smoking cannabis.

Mia leaned forward. "This conversation is over." She ended the call, then took a deep breath and directed her intense gaze on Liam. "I'm going to stay here in Magpie for a few days as this develops. You are to have no contact with your father. He's still a person of interest. He claims Derek Sexton was stealing the pensions, but we only have his word for that. I'll be at the Charm Hotel up by the highway. If anyone involved in this case gets in touch with you, call me."

CHAPTER NINETEEN

Liam had cooked them breakfast again. George wasn't used to a big meal at the beginning of the day, but having gone without regular meals for most of her childhood, she wasn't going to complain. She rinsed off her non-stick frying pan, dried it, and stowed it in the cupboard where it belonged. It was only fair that she wash the dishes seeing as he had taken over the responsibility of cooking. A situation which suited her. She had no patience for the culinary arts. Give her a cheese sandwich, and she was good to go.

After the excitement of yesterday, they'd spent a quiet evening streaming a movie. Then they'd gone to bed. Initially, they pretended they wanted to sleep. Well, maybe he had planned on sleeping, but she had other ideas. It had only taken a kiss for him to come around to her way of thinking.

She decided to forgo her morning exercise routine and read some of Davis' articles instead. She hadn't slept well. The idea that he might do a negative piece on her had played on her mind. He could write whatever he wanted. That was out of her control, but she should at least prepare herself for the fallout.

"Hey babe, when was the last time you checked your car?" Liam called from the open front door.

She walked to the living room so she wouldn't have to shout. He stood at the front door, wearing a torn, grease-stained UBC T-shirt, which revealed his abs.

"Two months ago." She didn't add that she couldn't bear to go near her car because then she would be forced to face the reality that she was no longer allowed to drive. It was a reminder of the freedom she'd lost when she'd had her seizure.

"Weren't you and Buddy going to look at it yesterday?" Now that she thought about it, he'd asked for her keys, but he hadn't given her an update on its status. With everything that had happened, it had completely slipped her mind.

"Buddy didn't have time." He crooked his finger, beckoning her closer. Once she was within arm's length, he grabbed her waist and pulled her into his embrace. "I'll see you in a while. I'm taking it to his house."

She laughed and then said, "Are you getting engine oil on my clean clothes?"

"Yes, they're dirty. You should take them off." He waggled his eyebrows.

She trailed a finger through the slit in his shirt, enjoying the feel of his warm skin over his toned muscles. "You first."

His phone buzzed in his pocket. He looked at the screen and then groaned. "Buddy says he has to work in an hour so I'm to get my pretty-boy ass in gear."

"He did not say 'pretty-boy ass.'"

"He did, look." He turned the phone toward her so she could read the text.

She hummed. "You do have a pretty ass. Should I be worried that Buddy's noticed it too?"

He winked at her. "It's all yours, babe." Then he turned and headed for her old Subaru in the driveway.

After he left, she made herself comfortable on the couch with her feet up. Time for some reading. She opened her laptop and worked through the process of paying for a subscription to Private Source News so she could access Jeff Davis' articles. Davis' bio said he was from Nova Scotia and that Private Source News had their head office in Ottawa. They were a well-respected national publication. The first piece she read was an exposé on organized crime and the construction industry. It was a heavy, hard-hitting column, which was strong on evidence. What kind of piece would he write on her? All of his articles were about crime, not fluffy human-interest editorials.

She opened another window on her screen and did a search for robberies. She needed to know if Davis used burglaries to collect his information. Thirty minutes later, she was still sifting through the data, but it was apparent that most of Davis' stories coincided with some kind of break-in.

Someone hammered on her front door. She jumped at the sound, made her way across the room, and peeked through the etched glass panel. Andrea stood on her porch, staring back at her.

What the hell was she doing here? George reached for her baseball bat just in case. Maybe if she started the conversation with a show of strength, Andrea might decide to leave.

As George slid the bolt into the unlock position, Andrea shoved at the door, slamming it open.

George jumped back. "What the h—!"

"Where's Liam?" Andrea shouted, stomping into the living room.

"Get out." George held her bat with both hands.

Andrea swung around, her blond hair flying about her face. "I've had enough of you spending time with my man." Her hands balled into fists.

The words "my man" echoed in George's head. They were proprietary, suggesting ownership. The hairs on the back of George's neck prickled, warning her that something was off. How was this the same woman who'd walked with her in Banff? That person had been shallow and materialistic, but at the same time she'd seemed devastated by the loss of a friend. The woman standing before her was aggressive and unhinged. She wasn't carrying a purse. She wore designer sweatpants and a tank top, which wouldn't hamper her movements. Maybe she was dressed to fight.

"He's not 'your man.'" George closed the distance between them.

"And you think he's yours?" Andrea pointed a finger at her. Her long talons were painted a sparkly gold color.

"No, I think he's his own man, and he's free to come and go as he pleases." George held the bat high, making sure Andrea had seen it.

Andrea crossed her arms. "We made a commitment to each other."

George said nothing to that pronouncement. She had no idea if anything had happened between them.

"We got matching tattoos. Do you have a tattoo?" Andrea pulled the strap of her tank top aside to reveal a small Celtic knot on her collar bone. It was exactly the same as Liam's except smaller.

George stepped closer, taking a long look before she said, "Interesting." A slow smile spread across her face. "Do you wanna see my tattoo? It's on my butt, and it says *You're a liar.*"

Andrea gasped. "How dare—?"

"The skin around your ink is red and raised. That's fresh. I don't know what game you're playing, but you'd better leave." George raised her bat.

"You can't talk to me— Are you threatening to hit me? I have a lawyer who'll sue—"

"What are you talking about? I'm just showing you this great bat. It has awesome balance. It's not my fault you got in the way when I was showing you how to use it." She did a few practice swings like a batter stepping up to the plate.

"I'm rich. I have—"

"I'm a cop," George shouted, her patience exhausted. She poked Andrea in the shoulder with the cap end of the bat. "You forced your way into my house, looking for trouble." Using her position to intimidate Andrea was wrong, but she was done letting this rich woman play mind games. It was time to put her on the defense. "What happened between you and Justin Cross? Were you having an affair?"

Andrea paled, her hand flying to her throat. She yelped, then turned and ran out of the house and down the driveway to her Porsche, which was parked on the road.

George stared after her. There was something so deranged about the whole scene that had just played out in her living room. The tattoo, the outrage, everything was so over the top. Andrea was obviously desperate, but why?

As disturbing as it had been, Andrea's act had revealed one detail. She had been having an affair with the deceased.

George closed and locked her door. Then she fished her phone out of her backpack and dialed Sergeant Olsen's number. The RCMP would want to know about this.

CHAPTER TWENTY

Derek Sexton took a sip of his coffee without tasting it. He'd followed his idiot daughter to this godforsaken town in an effort to stop her doing more damage. Unfortunately, Andrea was just like her mother. She thought if she created enough drama, people would get so distracted they would forget the original issue. Which in this case was who had a motive to kill Justin Cross.

He didn't give a shit that she'd been having an affair with Cross. He also didn't think she had the balls to kill him. Maybe Ella Mason was sleeping with him, too, and William had found out. He didn't know who'd killed the disloyal son-of-a-bitch, and he didn't care. As long as no one found out about his little money trouble, he was in the clear.

"I want the money by nine tomorrow morning." Davis tapped the table with his index finger.

"And if I don't?" Derek eyed the reporter. There were always people who saw him as an easy target—a soft, older man who was jovial and friendly. He didn't mind. He'd worked hard to cultivate that image because there were too many people in the business world who thought being nice implied weakness. Fostering the illusion meant he was continually underestimated. Sooner or later, his adversaries showed themselves, allowing him to pick them off. He loved nothing more than going in for the kill, both literally and figuratively. He simply enjoyed the carnage.

"The story of how you stole your employee's pensions will be made public." The scruffy reporter obviously thought he had the upper hand. He had an unkempt beard and the dishevelled fair hair of a beach bum. He was young and strong. The muscles on his arms and shoulders suggested he had good upper-body strength.

"I thought you were into exposing corruption, not blackmail." Derek had agreed to meet Davis because he wanted to know how much the idiot had on him.

"That was before Justin died."

Derek blinked and then laughed. It was good when things finally made sense. "You're the burglar. How did it work?" He put a hand to his head. "Let me guess. You break in and pretend to rob the place, but really you were there to meet Justin. Why the elaborate plan? Is a dark alley not good enough for you?"

"Some of my contacts fear for their lives. Apparently, Justin was right to be scared."

"How do you know I didn't kill him?"

"I've seen the police report. Your movements were accounted for—"

"You've seen the police—? Interesting." Derek would've liked to see the fear in Davis' eyes when he killed him, but that wasn't possible. By the look of his physique, Davis was too strong. Derek wouldn't be able to win. He would have to attack from behind in a fast, accurate strike.

"I never reveal a source. Now, about the money." Davis' back was rigid, and his tone was stern and threatening. He was probably trying to sound tough, but it just made him seem more desperate.

"How do I know you didn't kill Justin?" Derek made his voice warble as if he were scared.

Davis shrugged, shaking his head. "I didn't kill him, but I can't prove it. That's why I need the money. I have to get away."

"I will need everything you've got." Derek made sure his hands shook as he lifted his coffee cup.

Davis held up a red and gold USB drive. "This is all I got from Justin. There are no other copies."

"H-h-how do I know I can trust you?" It took all of Derek's self-control not to laugh in the reporter's face.

"I guess you don't, but if you don't pay me the money, I will publish my story, and you will be in the frame for murder as well as stealing the pension fund. It's your choice." Davis took a sip of his coffee, trying to seem nonchalant. "Pay me and buy yourself some time or do prison time for theft and maybe murder."

"You're just trying to scare me. I didn't kill Justin. You said so yourself. The police already suspect you."

Davis leaned forward and whispered, "Once the police find out the reason I was there to meet him, suspicion will fall on you."

There was a flaw in Davis' argument. Derek had an alibi, and he hadn't killed Justin. There was no way the police would suspect him. Unfortunately, he couldn't risk Davis' going to the RCMP with proof that he'd stolen money from the pension fund. No, Davis wouldn't do that. He was the kind of journalist who lived for the next sensational story. He would take the money and then write his article anyway.

Derek stood. "I see. It'll have to be a money order. Banks don't carry cash like they used to. I'll make the arrangements now."

He strolled to his Bugatti Divo sports car. It was a limited-edition vehicle that he rarely drove. He got in and dug his hunting knife out of the glove compartment and placed it under his seat. Then he fished his phone from his jacket pocket and pretended to be talking on it. He watched as Davis climbed into his beat-up Honda Accord.

He threw his phone onto the passenger seat as Davis reversed out of his parking spot and drove away. Derek slipped his car into gear and followed. There was no way he'd let a nobody like Davis ruin all his plans.

CHAPTER TWENTY-ONE

Liam had enjoyed spending time with Buddy, which was a surprise considering Georgina's friend had started their meeting by holding a large wrench to his throat and threatening to beat him if he was using her.

He had managed to convince Buddy that his intentions were honorable. After that, they'd set to work on her Subaru. Buddy figured the ball joints needed to be replaced in the front end. Liam took him at his word. He knew how to check the oil and washer fluid, but that was the extent of his mechanical expertise.

Georgina was almost vibrating with anger when he got home. Luckily, she'd stowed the baseball bat by the door. "Who would go to all the trouble of getting a tattoo to undermine our relationship?"

"I can't imagine." He felt sick to his stomach. Andrea was playing some kind of mind game. How could he prove she was lying? "My family and the Sextons went on a trip to Harrison Hot Springs, and I haven't seen her since."

Georgina stopped and stared at him. "When was this?"

He shrugged. "I don't know…about twelve years ago. I was on a break from university. Why?" His heart pounded. He had no idea if she believed him, but he could tell she was still angry by the way she clenched her jaw.

Her brow furrowed. "Am I right in assuming you had your tattoo when you went on this trip and she saw you shirtless? Were photos taken?"

"Yes, yes and yes. We stayed at the resort. It's luxurious. Everyone spent some time in the hot spring pool. My tattoo was new then. My dad didn't approve, but that was okay because I didn't rate him much either. I swear there's never been anything between me and Andrea."

She gave him a look that suggested he was crazy. "I know."

"You do?" He felt weak with relief.

"Of course." She continued to pace around the room, but her posture was more relaxed than it had been a few minutes ago. "Her tattoo was fresh. She just got it, which was fast. We left Banff on Sunday afternoon. It's now Tuesday, which means she got inked sometime in the last day and a half. This is so calculated. It's cruel, but it's also calculated," she repeated. Then she said, "The question is why. Why does she feel the need to do this?"

"I've said it before." He stood just inside the front door with his hands on his hips. He ached to take her in his arms but knew this wasn't the time. She needed to puzzle through this for her own peace of mind. "When you asked if the robbery and homicide were two separate incidents, it scared them."

She stopped in front of him and tilted her head. "It scared Andrea."

Liam's phone gave a piercing trill. "That's Mia." He'd allocated his boss the most annoying ringtone he could find.

"Jeff Davis has been found dead in his hotel room," she snapped, not wasting time.

Liam put the phone on speaker. "How was Davis killed?"

Georgina put a hand over her mouth, her eyes wide with shock.

"His throat was slit," Mia said.

He was surprised that she'd shared that much detail. "Is there anything else?"

"His laptop and phone are missing."

"Did you find a red and gold memory stick?" Georgina asked, her face pale.

"The crime scene techs are still going through the room. I'll make sure they look for it." Mia hung up.

"I wasn't expecting that." Georgina blew out a long breath.

"Me either," he agreed. "You need to be prepared. Davis was in Magpie to write a story on you."

She collapsed onto the couch. "And I didn't want that."

"Exactly, which means you're a suspect."

CHAPTER TWENTY-TWO

"Hi." George approached Carly, a former waitress at the Rockin Horse, who now worked in housekeeping at the Charm Hotel. The short, curvy young woman wore her shoulder-length hair tied up in a messy ponytail. Now that the bar was closed, she'd found employment cleaning rooms for the summer.

"Hi." Carly narrowed her eyes as George approached, the young woman's suspicion apparent.

"Look, I have no right to ask…" George left the rest of her question unspoken, hoping Carly would fill in the blanks.

"You want access to the room where the guy was killed." Carly consulted her clipboard and wheeled her big yellow cart to the next room in the long, dim hallway.

George winced. "Am I that obvious?"

"Yes, you are." She stopped and flashed her card in front of the electronic lock, which made a click. "Do they have a suspect?" She opened the door.

"As far as I can tell, they think I did it," George stated baldly. Sergeant Olsen had arrived, unannounced, on George's doorstep three hours ago and interrogated her extensively on her dealings with Jeff Davis. She had answered the questions honestly, leaving nothing out. She'd even told the sergeant how she'd stolen the memory stick.

Once Sergeant Olsen was gone, Liam had persuaded George to check out the room where Davis had died. It hadn't taken much to get her to agree.

Carly sighed and tugged the lanyard with the key attached over her head. "You've given me some good advice about school, and my former boss did try to kill you, so I figure I owe you."

"Thanks." George grinned, putting her hands together in a prayer motion, signaling her appreciation. She ran along the corridor to Liam, who was waiting at room one-zero-three, opened the door, and then returned the key to Carly.

She joined Liam, standing at the threshold, peering into the room. It had been roughly twenty-four hours since Jeff Davis' body had been found. He would've been taken to the medical examiner. The crime scene techs had gone over every inch and taken anything they believed was relevant to the case.

Liam crossed the room, stopping near the bathroom. "That's a lot of blood." He pointed to the red splotch on the carpet near the door.

The room was surprisingly spartan given that the Charm Hotel was the most luxurious hotel in town. It held one queen bed, two nightstands, and a dresser with a TV on top.

"Yes, it is." Sergeant Olsen's commanding voice resonated through the hotel corridor. "What the hell do you two think you're doing?"

Shit. George slowly turned to face the RCMP officer who stood with her arms folded across her chest. She must have a stealth mode because she'd managed to creep up on them in silence.

"This is down to me." Liam moved to stand next to George. "You questioned Georgina as if she were guilty. I wanted to see the scene for myself. Am I right in assuming his throat was slit from behind?"

The sergeant sighed. "I guess there's no harm seeing as we've finished with the scene and taken all the evidence." She pushed past George and Liam, pacing to the other side of the bed.

From her position at the door, George stared at the layer of fingerprint powder that covered the nightstand. "I take it the memory stick is missing." There was no way she could look at Jeff's blood. She hadn't liked him, but knowing his young life had been cut short was hard to take.

"Yes, along with his computer and laptop." Sergeant Olsen stared out of the window, not looking at the blood either.

"Did you find the jewels that were stolen from the house in Banff? George asked, scanning the corridor for security cameras, rather than looking at the horror show in the hotel room.

"How did you know?" Olsen demanded.

"I'll tell you later. That's it for me." There was no way George could stay. The repulsive smell of Davis' death was getting to her. "There's a coffee shop in the lobby. I'll meet you there."

"Wait," Sergeant Olsen commanded.

She stopped in her tracks and turned to see Olsen standing in the hallway. Her eyes narrowed. "What kind of a police officer are you?"

"I'm a community cop. I deal with small crime only. I had to handle a stabbing victim once. Luckily, he was still alive." George turned on her heel and headed to the foyer. A coffee might steady her nerves.

She purchased a drink and sat at a table by the window. This café was more upscale than Olivia's place with plush leather chairs and varnished wood tables. There was a time when she'd stopped here every day when on patrol. She perused the coffee shop, no cameras, but she had noticed some in the reception area.

Liam and Olsen joined her a few minutes later.

Sergeant Olsen sat down while Liam dragged over another chair. Neither of them ordered a drink. George wished Olsen would head back to her regular job in Edmonton. No such luck.

"This is a nice place," Sergeant Olsen said, taking in the stylish surroundings.

"I thought so. I used to come here all the time. Actually, I had my seizure right there." She pointed to a spot near the counter.

Liam winced. "Don't remind me." He had been with her at the time, posing as a rookie with the Magpie Police Service.

Sergeant Olsen stared at George. "I was hoping for your insight."

"Me?" George couldn't contain her surprise. This was way out of her league.

"Yes, you." Olsen pointed at her. "Tell me how you knew we'd find the jewels?"

"It was just a guess. Look Sergeant, I'm just making—"

"Call me Mia."

"Okay, Mia... Before I start, I need to tell you I was wrong about the burglaries in Banff being connected to houses for sale.

Or maybe not entirely wrong." She rubbed her neck as she tried to organize her thoughts. "I honestly don't know for sure, but I don't think Davis was responsible for them. I think he just robbed Sexton's house."

"But they all have the same M.O."

"Yes, they do. But similar crimes have taken place all over the country. Maybe Davis figured out the pattern and copied it as a means to get the information he needed for his stories."

"Are you telling me they're not connected? And I'm wasting man hours on that?" Mia's eyes flashed with anger.

George could feel her face heat. She'd made an assumption, and she'd been wrong. There was nothing she could do to correct her mistake except own it. "Maybe some of them are. I don't really know anything for certain. Davis did rob Sexton's house in Banff. The jewels prove that. I just don't think he robbed all the houses in the area."

Mia pursed her lips as she considered George's words and then said, "Explain how you knew he would have the stolen goods."

"There were two things that pointed to Davis being the robber. The first was the jewels. Derek Sexton said he normally kept them in the safe but stuffed them in the linen closet because he was busy. So why did the thief look there unless he already knew where to find the valuables?"

Mia tugged her notepad out of her purse and scribbled the details. "What was the second thing?"

"Davis' actions. He approached me in the park. He wasn't on my radar. I'd never seen him before. It was he who suggested that the robbery and the homicide were two different crimes. Why would he even consider that unless he was there? I think Davis staged the robbery to get the info. I believe it was some kind of handoff. But someone killed Justin before he got there."

"And he knew they were separate felonies because he was the burglar," Mia finished.

"Exactly. I suspect you'll find that's how Davis protected his sources. He'd sneak into an informant's house. He collects the evidence and takes a few valuables. The leak can be explained by the robberies so there's no risk to the whistleblower. I made a start on cross-referencing his stories with reported burglaries, but you have the resources to do the job properly."

George glanced at Liam. He sat with his arms crossed, stone-faced. There was nothing in his demeanour that suggested he was going to voice an opinion anytime soon.

"And he knew where the jewels were because his informant had told him. Is that why you copied the memory stick? How'd you know it was important?" Mia persisted.

"It's like I told you this morning, I heard him talking to some-one." George closed her eyes, picturing the moment in the Jumping Bean when she'd approached Davis. "He said, 'In two days this story will be published unless we can come to an arrangement.' That sounded like blackmail to me."

"But how did you know the USB drive was important?" Mia asked for the umpteenth time.

George sighed. "Everything I've told you about my actions on that day are born out of instinct and supposition. I don't know anything for sure. I couldn't steal his laptop or phone. He would've noticed. The stick was there, so I grabbed it, not that it can be used as evidence for the prosecution. I'm aware that a good lawyer would have any information from a stolen memory stick thrown out of court. If the attorney was really aggressive, they might use the manner in which I acquired the information to cast doubt on your whole case."

Mia nodded. "I understand. For the record, Liam's father has provided us with documentation that confirms everything that was on that USB drive. He also has a recording of Sexton black-mailing him in order to get Mr. Mason to transfer the pension funds into Sexton's account. That's proof we can use. Your in-stincts were spot on."

Liam let out a long breath, a small sign he was relieved. If she hadn't been watching him for a reaction, she might have missed it.

George shrugged. "It's not rocket science. Whoever killed Jeff Davis also took his laptop, phone, and the memory stick. To me, that suggests blackmail. What do you think?"

"The same," Liam said, finally contributing to the conversation. "Can we also assume that whoever killed Justin also murdered Davis?"

"I'm not sure." George pictured the office and the side table with the blood. "I just..." She bit her lip as she thought through everything that had happened since Friday. "I think you need to find Andrea Sexton and question her."

CHAPTER TWENTY-THREE

George smiled when Liam placed a mug of steaming coffee on the nightstand next to her. She'd woken to the sound of him in the shower and decided to lie in bed. She relished the joy of having him in her life. He'd been back for a week, and every day was better than the last.

"Good morning, sleepy." His hair was still damp, and he smelled of soap and his own unique scent that always gave her butterflies in her stomach. He wore a pair of cargo pants and no shirt.

She stacked her pillows behind her as she sat up. "You spoil me." She held the mug in both hands and took a sip, savoring the aromatic, slightly bitter taste of hot coffee and the way it slid down her dry throat.

The bed sagged as he joined her against the headboard. He stretched out his long legs in front of him. He took a swallow from his own cup and then said, "I do everything the same as you, but my coffee is never as good."

"There's a secret."

"What's that?"

"Food, and in this case, coffee is always better if someone else makes it." She grinned.

He placed his drink on the nightstand and said, "We need to talk."

"Oh, God." She didn't have much experience with relationships, but even she knew those words were always followed by bad news.

He held up his hands in a halt motion. "Nothing bad. At least, I hope it's not bad for you."

She didn't like the way he was hedging. "Just tell me." Her nerves were getting to her. Had he changed his mind about staying and decided to leave?

"I wanted to have this conversation sooner, but my mom called and then…" He shrugged. "You know the rest."

"What is it?" No one would ever describe her as patient.

"I want us to be an item. I want this to go somewhere."

"Where?" She blinked, dumbfounded by her own stupid question. She hadn't expected him to say that. She'd asked herself the same thing the morning after his return but hadn't been brave enough to raise the subject.

He crossed and uncrossed his legs. "I don't know. I guess I want us to spend time together and see if it could work. I'm not playing around. For me, this is serious."

"Me, too." She set her mug down. Straddling him, she gave him a quick kiss. Before he could react, she brushed a strand of his dark hair away from his forehead. Then she laid a hand on his pecs, enjoying the feel of his chest hair under her fingertips. "I want you to stay. I love having you here." She stared over his head. He had been honest with her. She needed to find the courage to tell him how she felt. "I hate the thought of you going away or being transferred, but we'll make it work—"

"About that…"

"What?" She tilted back on her heels, assessing him.

His gaze connected with hers. "The job of police chief with the Magpie Police Service is still up for grabs." He'd told her when he'd first returned that he was done with the RCMP but hadn't mentioned it since.

"And you're considering it?"

"Yes. They called me. But if you don't think it will work. If you think—"

"That would be awesome. I know you're burnt out with the RCMP, but are you sure you'll be happy here?"

He grinned as his big, warm hand rubbed her knee. "You inspired me."

"I did?"

"Yes. Being a community cop is important. You've really made a difference in the lives of the people here. I want to be part of a community. I want to be a cop like you."

She climbed off his lap and moved back to her original position, leaning against the headboard. She missed his touch, but it was distracting, and she needed to think. "If you do get the job, that'll make you my boss. How will that work?"

"I don't know. I haven't had a chance to consider all the ramifications." He sat up so he was facing her. "If you don't want me to go for it, or if you don't think it'll work, then tell me now. I'll find something else. I can stay in the RCMP and give up undercover work." But if he stayed with the Mounties, he could be posted anywhere in Canada.

"Honestly, you can't include my work in the equation. I don't know what I'm doing with my life. I don't know if I even want to be a cop anymore." Especially since she had only joined the Magpie Police Service to stop her father, who was now in jail. "I don't even know if I should stay in this house or move into town. But I do know I like being with you. Your happiness is important to me. If working for the Magpie Police Service will make you happy, then you should do it."

He shifted off the bed. "I'd better leave. I have a meeting with the mayor and the town council at ten."

"You have an interview?" She couldn't keep the surprise out of her voice.

"John called me when you were in bed this morning. He asked me if I was interested."

"He called you? You didn't apply for this job?" She knew she was parroting his words but couldn't help it.

"Yes, he said the council have been looking for someone who would be a good fit." He kissed her and then tugged on his white button-down shirt. "I wish I'd packed my suit. I would've gotten a haircut if I'd have known I'd be going for an interview."

"Tell them you were working undercover. It'll be a conversation starter and possibly the most exciting thing they've heard since the armored car robbery."

He headed for the living room. "Wish me luck."

She heard the jangle of car keys. "Good luck. Meet me at the Jumping Bean when you're done," she called as he closed the front door.

She smiled as she headed to the shower. He wanted to stay.

CHAPTER TWENTY-FOUR

Derek Sexton followed the road along the lakeshore until it became a muddy trail. He slowed the car, looking for an isolated spot. He needed to find a place where he could dump the clothes he'd been wearing when he killed Davis, along with the knife, memory stick, computer, and phone. Away from the town, it was quiet except for the birds. The sun had just risen. The waterfowl were celebrating the morning by squawking loud enough to drown out an orchestra.

He cursed as he hit a bump in the road and bounced to the left. The racing suspension on his Bugatti was not made for dirt tracks, or hick towns for that matter. He corrected and carried on driving.

Killing Davis had been grislier than he'd expected. He had no idea it would be so messy. Davis wasn't the first person he'd murdered. He was the second. But poisoning a rival was a clean, clinical way to get rid of someone. Using his knife had been messy and had left too much evidence. Oh, well, lesson learned. Next time he would be smarter.

Luckily, he'd managed to grab Davis from behind, and most of the splatter had been directed away from him. He'd originally taken everything to his room on the second floor of the Charm Hotel, just to get it out of sight. Everyone knew there were cameras in the elevators, but he was fit enough that taking the stairs wasn't a hardship. He'd planned to stow the proof of his crime in a plastic garbage bag in the trunk of the car and dump it in the mountains on the way home. But he'd woken in the middle of the night with the terrible feeling he'd missed something, some important detail. An internet search revealed that police forensics were a lot more meticulous than he'd imagined. Apparently, they could extract DNA from a microscopic trace of organic matter. And no matter how well he thought he'd cleaned his knife, there were probably still tiny droplets of Davis' blood under the hilt.

The road widened, giving him enough room to pull over. This seemed like a great spot to make his bag of goodies disappear. Was he far enough out of town? Maybe he should continue on, but he didn't want to wreck his car. If the low-riding Bugatti got stuck and he had to call a tow truck, it would be game over. He might be able to explain why he'd driven off-road in a priceless vehicle, but it would attract unwanted attention.

When he parked, he spied a young family in a small aluminium boat about fifty yards out. *Damn it.* He steered onto the trail and kept going.

The police were bound to question him. He'd met Davis in a coffee-shop. They'd been seen. There were cameras everywhere these days. He was surprised the cops hadn't already contacted him. Why hadn't he left the moment he'd killed the blackmailing bastard? Because he hadn't wanted to draw attention to himself. He was a concerned father, looking for his daughter who'd gone off the deep end. Yeah, the police would buy that. Although the truth was he'd stopped looking for Andrea the minute Davis had called with his demand. As long as he got rid of the evidence, he was in the clear. Luckily, this backwater town sat on the edge of a big-ass lake.

He drove along the rutted dirt road. This wasn't a manicured shoreline. It was muddy with tall reeds and murky water. He scanned the area. There was no one about. He carried on driving, checking the vicinity. After another few minutes he came to a small house with a bright blue bike chained to the deck. The road ahead was in worse condition than the trail he had just traveled. Large boulders with sharp edges stuck out of the compacted ruts, and deep trenches crisscrossed the roadway where stormwater had drained into the lake. There was no way his Bugatti could handle those conditions. He made a U-turn. The stretch of shoreline between the house and the family in the boat would have to work. He parked on a patch of dried mud by the shore.

He gathered a few rocks, which were lying on the rough ground, opened the trunk, and added them to the bag. He tied the ends, making sure it wouldn't come undone. With the evidence in hand, he prepared for the throw, winding his arm, intending to hurl it as far as he could. He stopped. What if it got snagged by a fisherman? He twisted to his left and flung it into the reeds. Birds flew up into the air, squawking with fright, roused by the bag landing close by. He stood staring at the spot, breathing easily for the first time since he'd realized his blunder.

"Are you Derek Sexton?"

He froze. The question sent a chill down his spine.

He turned to see a small blond woman walking toward him. She wore leggings, a T-shirt, and had a runner's pouch attached to a belt at her waist. "I'm Sergeant Olsen with the RCMP." She pulled out her identification.

Shit, shit, shit. She'd seen him. There was no doubt that she would be able to pinpoint where he had dumped the evidence.

"Yes, I'm Sexton. What can I do for you?" He smiled, falling back on the fake persona he'd cultivated over the years. All he had to do was keep calm. She was alone. He was bigger and stronger. It wouldn't be hard to overpower her. He could dump her body here in the lake.

"I was just passing." She pointed to the muddy roadway. "I saw you and thought I recognized the face. What brings you out here?"

He glanced around, looking for an answer. He just had to keep her talking until an opportunity opened up. "The ducks."

"You came all the way out here to feed the ducks?" Her eyes widened. She didn't believe him.

He smiled, hoping it seemed genuine. "Isn't this off the beaten track for a jog?"

She raised her eyebrows as if deciding whether to answer and then said, "I was going to see a friend, who I've been told makes a good cup of coffee."

He nodded, trying to seem congenial. "I needed a relaxing place to think. My daughter hasn't been herself lately. I followed her here. I'm worried about her. Have you heard about Justin Cross?"

"Why don't you tell me?" She folded her arms across her chest.

"He died during a robbery. She hasn't taken it well. I didn't realize they were involved, or I would've said something." He sighed, hoping it conveyed sympathy. "He was married, you see. Now I'm scared she'll do something rash." He just had to play the concerned parent for a minute longer.

"Like what?" She hadn't moved. Hadn't shown any sign that she suspected him in Davis' homicide.

"Who knows? She seems obsessed with Liam and his girlfriend. I have no idea why." He bent down near a hand-sized rock, pretending to tie his shoelace.

Her phone vibrated. While she pulled the device from her belt and read the text, he grabbed the rock.

She dismissed whatever message she'd read. "Do you know where your—"

He spun as fast as he could and aimed the rock at her head. She blocked him with her left arm. He slammed it down again, trying to hit her head. She cried out in pain as the rock pounded her forearm. She punched him in the ribs with her free hand. The blow made him buckle at the waist. He dropped the rock and rushed at her, ramming into her, using his weight to knock her off her feet. They landed on the ground with her beneath him. She struck him, hitting his cheek.

He shifted so his knees were on either side of her chest. "Stay still, bitch." He grabbed her by the throat and squeezed.

CHAPTER TWENTY-FIVE

George dropped her bike and was running before it hit the ground. Derek Sexton sat on Mia Olsen's chest while he choked her. Olsen hammered on his hands with her fists, trying to break his hold.

As soon as she was within reach, George dived, knocking Derek off Mia.

They landed with her sprawled lengthways on top of his body, her head smacked him in the ribs, her knees even with his shins.

He grabbed her waist and tried to roll so he would be on top. She remembered her jujitsu training and allowed him to push her onto her back. He tried to punch her. She blocked with her left elbow, then she hooked her legs around his waist, grabbed his body, and hugged him to her chest.

He continued to hit her, but from this angle all he could reach was her upper back. She weathered his blows as she adjusted position and hooked her legs around his neck. Then she grabbed his right arm and wrenched it between their bodies so it was jammed against his throat. He was immobilized. The more he struggled, the less he could breathe.

His faced turned bright red, whether from anger or loss of air she wasn't sure. But she couldn't let go until he was no longer a threat.

She glanced at Mia who sat a few feet away. "Are you okay?"

"Yes," she croaked, rubbing her neck.

"Call for backup."

Mia nodded and crawled across the ground to where her phone lay in the dirt.

Derek tried to heave himself up and escape George's hold.

"Stop moving," she growled.

"Breathe," Derek panted, tapping her leg.

She loosened her grip, allowing Derek to fall to the ground. She rolled to a standing position and stood over him, watching for any sign that he might strike her. Sirens sounded in the distance. The cavalry was coming.

Mia gained her feet and staggered over to George. "I was about to ask him to come in for questioning." She was still breathless, and her neck was red from where Sexton had attacked her, but she was holding her own.

George cast her gaze over Derek. He was still lying on the ground, but he wasn't gasping or in distress.

The Magpie Police car pulled up beside them, its lights flashing.

George's arm jerked uncontrollably. Her whole body tingled. The smell of burning toast was overwhelming. "No." She forced the word out. She felt as if she were floating through space.

"Georgina?" Mia called her, but it sounded far away.

She tried to turn and answer, but her responses were in slow motion as if she were looking down on the scene through a fog, and her damn arm was still spasming.

Then everything was normal. The world came into focus. It was as though someone had flicked a switch, making her able to respond again. The episode, or whatever it was, was over. "I'm fine."

Officer Alan Hammond and Greg Nicholson were cuffing Derek Sexton and reading him his rights. Both were colleagues and friends. Greg nodded her way. "Are you okay?

"Fine," she murmured. It was an automatic response.

Mia grabbed her arm and led her away from the chaos. "I think you just had a seizure. You need to rest." She shoved George down on the ground, forcing her to sit. "Don't look at the flashing lights. I'll call Liam."

She left George and joined Hammond and Nicholson at the cruiser. As an RCMP member, who was also the victim of an attack, Mia would have to file a report, and she probably needed medical attention. George wanted to help but did as she was told and stayed with her back to her fellow officers.

She had no idea what charges would be leveled against Derek Sexton. Mia's superiors in Edmonton might get involved. If asked,

George would tell them what she knew, what she suspected, and what she'd witnessed.

She looked out over the lake. A couple of ducks swam by. One of them dived for food, oblivious to the drama on shore. Or maybe human drama didn't matter as long as they had food and shelter.

Had the flashing lights caused another seizure? Maybe, but she'd been conscious this time. She'd known what was happening, but her brain had hijacked her body. There'd been that freaky twitchy arm thing and the smell of burning toast. She hadn't been able to stop it or pull herself out. Worst of all, it had happened in front of an RCMP sergeant. There was no way she would ever be a cop again.

CHAPTER TWENTY-SIX

Liam placed a cup of coffee on the table beside George, then sat on the couch and wrapped his arms around her, tucking her head into his shoulder.

She'd been checked out at the hospital. Dr. Sullivan had put her on anti-seizure medication, had made an appointment for her with a neurologist, and sent her home.

Liam didn't say anything, which was good because she didn't want to hear platitudes like everything will be fine or we'll figure this out. In time, she would be okay, but at the moment she was devastated. It wasn't that her job with the Magpie Police Service was over; she'd been emotionally preparing for a change in careers. Police work had never been her calling. She'd enjoyed the difference she'd made in the community of Magpie, but she'd never thought of it as something she would do until she retired. What devastated her was having epilepsy and being banned from driving. It meant a total lifestyle change, one that had been a possibility but was now a reality.

A knock sounded at the door.

Liam kissed her head and then rose and answered it.

"Hi." Mia stood at the threshold. "Can I have a word with Georgina?"

Liam turned to her for guidance.

"Sure." Talking to Mia might be a welcome change from wallowing in self-pity.

"Coffee?" Liam motioned for his boss to sit.

"Sure." She flopped down in the armchair. Ugly black and purple bruises covered her neck. One was even in the shape of a thumb. It revealed just how much pressure Derek Sexton had been applying.

"How are you? Did they check you out?" George asked.

"I've just come from the hospital. There's no lasting damage. I

110

thought I'd give you an update and thank you for...well, for intervening."

"Anyone would've done the same."

Mia nodded, accepting George's answer. "I wanted to tell you we've arrested Derek Sexton for the murder of Jeff Davis and Justin Cross.

George sat up straight. "But that's wrong."

Liam passed Mia a mug and then frowned at George. "What do you mean?"

"I think Andrea killed Justin, but I don't think it was premeditated." George couldn't prove it, but it was the only answer that made sense.

"What?" Liam and Mia said in unison.

George rolled her eyes. "Okay, I'm only eighty percent certain." She waved her hands in a balancing motion. "Maybe ninety percent."

There was no table within reach, so Mia carefully placed her cup on the floor. "Tell me why you think Andrea killed Justin."

"For too long, I assumed she didn't like me because I was with Liam. But when we first arrived at the house in Banff, she appeared to be genuinely upset."

"I remember that. She looked like she'd been crying," Liam agreed.

"And she was friendly when I bumped into her shopping in Banff. We assumed that Justin was killed because he was passing information off to Davis, but what if it really was a horrible accident?" George gave them a second to absorb that piece of information and then continued, "There were only two people to leave the table. Your mom and Andrea."

"She said she went to the bathroom," Liam added.

"And at the time, she was so obviously upset I had no reason to doubt her." George stood and paced to the window, staring out over the lake.

"What changed your mind?" Mia asked.

George turned to face her. "When she came on to Liam in front of me, I mistakenly thought it was about Liam, but it wasn't. It was about distracting me."

She rubbed her forehead, getting it clear in her mind, and then addressed Liam. "You said you hadn't seen her in years. And as I said, this isn't the first relationship for either of us, so why would you lie about her? Plus, I trust you."

Liam smiled and blew her a kiss. Outwardly, he seemed relaxed, sitting on the couch, with his long legs crossed at the ankles, but there was a tenseness to him that suggested Andrea's actions had been too personal to dismiss.

Mia sighed. "This is all very sweet, but what made you think she killed Justin Cross?"

"To start, I believe Andrea and Justin were having an affair. Andrea told me he was kind to her. From the way she spoke, I suspect that her life hasn't been filled with an overabundance of kindness."

"That's sad, but it doesn't prove anything," Mia pointed out.

"True. We have no way of knowing how Justin felt, but I think Andrea was besotted."

"You mean it was a crime of passion?" Liam frowned, obviously unconvinced.

She pinched her lips together as she thought about how it could have happened. "This is just speculation. I haven't seen the autopsy. I don't know anything about the physical evidence. I'm just reading the behaviour of the people involved. This is, at best, a guess."

"Understood," Mia said with a curt nod.

George continued, "We know from Liam's dad that Justin was upstairs, waiting to pass off the information about the pension theft to Davis. I think Andrea saw him leave and thought she'd have a little rendezvous with her secret lover."

Liam grunted and then said, "That makes sense. He would be her type; his star was on the rise."

"Unless she confesses, there's no way to know if Justin told her what he was doing or if she figured it out. Maybe he simply tripped and hit his head. Whatever happened, she tried to cover it up. She overplayed her hand when she showed me her tattoo—"

"The one that matched mine." Liam scowled.

"It's like I told you, her skin was red, indicating it was fresh."

Mia tilted her head and frowned. "So, she got a tattoo to cause trouble between you and Liam to...?"

"To throw me off. Yes, that's exactly what I'm telling you. Liam, it was you who said the fact that the break-in and the homicide were two separate incidents really scared the people in that house."

"And you said it scared Andrea. I remember." He nodded, agreeing with her.

"She was desperate to distract me. But I don't see her as a cold-blooded killer. Whatever happened was an accident or a spur of the moment thing."

"And then Davis broke in and discovered the body." Liam patted the cushion next to him, silently asking her to sit.

She collapsed onto the couch, suddenly feeling exhausted. The events of the day were catching up with her. "Yes, and the red and gold memory stick, which suggests to me that Andrea didn't know about it. If she did, I think she would have taken it. Derek Sexton was set to bankroll her home staging business, and she would've wanted to protect that."

Mia picked her mug up off the floor. "Okay, I can buy that, and it actually tallies with our evidence." She gave George an appraising look. "How did Derek Sexton know about Davis?"

"I told you I overheard Davis blackmailing someone. I suspect Sexton was the person on the other end of the line. If you call the restaurants and coffee shops in the area, you might find someone who saw them together."

"Would they have met in a public place?" Mia asked. "Sexton wouldn't want to be seen."

"I doubt Sexton would've agreed to meet in public." Liam sounded skeptical.

George tapped his knee. "If Sexton didn't kill Justin, he might have suspected Davis of the crime. Davis probably felt the same —he didn't kill Justin, so he might've thought Sexton was guilty. There's no way these two could've trusted each other."

Mia took a long sip of her coffee. "In his initial police interview, Sexton claimed he didn't kill Justin, but he met with Davis and followed him back to his hotel room."

"Has he admitted to killing Davis?" Liam asked.

"Not yet."

"He slit Davis' throat. I'd put money on it. But he didn't expect all the blood splatter. He had to get rid of the knife, his clothes, and the stuff he'd stolen," Liam finished.

George blanched at the memory of the blood and death. "I can't wrap my head around Sexton's thinking. Did he follow his daughter here because he believed she killed Justin, or did he wonder why she was going off the deep end? And why didn't he just pay Davis off? Why kill him?"

They lapsed into silence.

Liam stood, retrieved the carafe from the kitchen, and filled Mia's coffee. He straightened suddenly and said, "Sexton could never have trusted a reporter like Davis. This was a man who was prepared to rob houses to get his stories. He probably lived for the next headline. Anyone who would go to such extremes couldn't be counted on to not publish."

Liam's comment reminded George of how she'd led the investigation astray. "Sorry about pointing you in the wrong direction with the burglaries in Banff. I got it wrong. Davis didn't rob them." George hated that she'd wasted the RCMP's resources.

Mia shrugged George's comment away and took a last sip of her coffee. "I didn't see Sexton throwing anything away when I was jogging along the lakeshore, but I did want to bring him in for questioning."

"And he attacked you." Liam returned the carafe to the kitchen.

"So, going back to the murder of Jeff Davis," Mia said, not letting the subject drop. "Sexton kills Davis' and then grabs his computer, phone, and memory stick. But we checked the cameras at the front desk and parking lot, looking for anyone leaving the hotel after the time of death." She stared into space.

Liam returned to his spot on the couch.

George put her hand in his, wishing this conversation was over and Mia would leave. "There are no cameras in the hallways of that hotel. I checked while you two were going over the room. The Charm Hotel is the best place in town. If Sexton was staying there, he could've used the stairs, and no one would've seen him."

Mia slumped back in her chair. She seemed exhausted, as though needing to know what happened and why she was attacked were the only things keeping her going. "The daughter killed her lover, and the father murdered a journalist. I have a team of divers searching the lake. Let's hope they come up with some evidence."

"I think once you question Andrea, she will admit the truth." George smiled.

Mia stood and headed for the door. "Do you know why I came to Magpie?" She wasn't the warm, fuzzy type, but she was forthright, a trait George appreciated.

Liam followed her. "To stop us interfering in an ongoing investigation."

She smiled. "That was what I told my superiors. I came here because of Georgina's intuition."

"Me? I don't know anything." George blinked.

Mia turned the handle of the door and then stopped. "It's just a theory, but I believe all that time you spent as a child watching your father deal drugs has given you an insight into the human condition that other people just don't have."

"Not that it'll do any good. I'm out of the force." The finality of those words was a gut-punch but not as devastating as she'd expected. She'd been injured on the job and been granted twenty-six weeks paid leave, which had started two months ago. She still had over four months to figure out what was next for her.

"I'll keep you informed of any developments. I'm going to be on leave myself for a few weeks." Mia waved and headed for her car.

"I hope you feel better," George called as she joined Liam on the deck to say goodbye.

He grinned as he watched Mia reverse out of the driveway. Then he threw an arm over her shoulder. "Good, now she's gone, we can talk."

"You got the job," George blurted.

Liam stared at her, open-mouthed. "How did you know?"

"I'm sorry. I didn't mean to steal your thunder."

He placed his hands on her waist and lifted her up in the air and twirled her around. "I'm the new police chief of the Magpie Police Service."

She didn't talk again until her feet touched the ground. "When did they tell you?"

"This morning as the interview concluded. I think they'd decided before I even got there." He seemed lighter as though a weight that had been sitting on his chest was now lifted.

"But that was hours ago. Why didn't you tell me earlier?"

He grimaced. "I felt bad being happy when you're going through so much. I was just about to tell you when Mia arrived."

"Don't feel bad. It's good to get out of my head and not think about my own predicament. And I'm happy for you." She wrapped her arms around his neck. The honesty of her words surprised her. The fact that things were working out for him made her feel better.

He pulled her close. "Things will turn around. One day soon, something good will come your way, and we'll be celebrating for you."

CHAPTER TWENTY-SEVEN

George sat on her deck, drinking her morning coffee. It had been two days since Derek Sexton had been detained. Hopefully, things would calm down now. Liam's mom, Ella, had called and apologized for her behaviour, explaining that she'd discovered Justin's role in exposing Sexton after she'd phoned Liam. She hadn't wanted to compromise his job with the RCMP. She'd used George's presence to drive him away.

George had accepted her apology. At the same time, she was thankful Liam's parents lived in a different province. She hadn't asked if William would keep his job with Starling Stores or what actions would be taken by the company. She didn't really understand high-finance and, more importantly, she didn't want to learn about it.

Liam sat in the chair next to her, resting his feet on the railing. "How was my mom?"

"Nice."

"A one-word answer. That's not very promising."

"It'll be good." She took a sip of her coffee, not tasting it. "At least, I hope it will. I promise, I'll always be nice to them."

"That's all I can ask, and probably more than they deserve." He reached over and placed a hand over hers. "I talked to Mia while you were on the phone. They've arrested Andrea."

"Where was she?"

"They caught her trying to cross the border into Montana."

"I wasn't expecting that. Has she been charged?"

"Yes, with manslaughter. She confessed. It was just as you said. She went upstairs to see Justin. He told her to leave. She thought he was seeing someone else. She hit him as hard as she could. He lost his balance, tripped and fell backward."

"He tripped?" She couldn't keep her skepticism out of her tone.

He frowned. "You were the one who suggested it was an accident."

"I did, but it's very anticlimactic when you consider she was making a run for the border."

He laughed, the sound warming her heart.

"You never said when you were starting your new job." She changed the subject to a more practical one.

"Even though I worked here for a couple of weeks in June, there's still a lot to learn. I'm going to go in and shadow a different department every day. I want to make sure I understand how it all works. Then Jake's promised to teach me the paperwork."

"Urgh." All cops hated the form-filling that was an essential part of the job.

"I was thinking. How about I rent a nice place in town, and you move in with me?"

"Are you sure?" They hadn't discussed their living situation. Initially, he'd planned to spend his vacation with her. Now that he was here fulltime, everything had changed.

"Yes. I know it's fast, but look at it like this." He poked the air with his index finger. "We'll be getting to know each other." Then he held up a second digit. "You won't be so far from everything so you can get around when it's cold." He gave up counting and made a sweeping motion that encompassed their surroundings. "It'll give you time to figure out what you want to do."

The wind rustled the trees and the lake rippled, lapping against the shore. She'd miss this place, but it was time to move on. She'd been fighting the change because it wasn't her idea. It was a situation born out of circumstance. But she wanted to be with Liam. If he had chosen to stay in the RCMP and was posted to Nunavut, the most northerly territory in Canada, she would've gone in a heartbeat. Living with Liam in Magpie would be a dream. One that she hoped would live up to its promise.

If you enjoyed Two For Joy
You can read other books in
The Magpie Romantic Suspense Mysteries

One For Sorrow
&
Three For a Girl

You might Also enjoy Marlow's
Gathering Storm Series

Sign up for Marlow's Newsletter to have
two Gathering Storm stories delivered to your inbox.
You'll also be notified of sales and new releases.
You can unsubscribe at any time.
https://www.subscribepage.com/marlowkelly

"THE CHEMISTRY BETWEEN THE MAIN CHARACTERS IS OUT OF THIS FREAKING WORLD!"

5 star
Amazon review for
Disturbance